WHAT'S
ON
THE
MENU?

Chase
Griffin

Opening Credits

Boring Stuff

Self-Promotion

WHAT'S ON THE MENU?

A Novel

Chase Griffin

Long Day Press

"I didn't know the questioner was a reporter, though I'm sure I would have answered the same even if I had."

—John Douglas, *Mindhunter*

CHAPTER ONE
Spinal Fluid for a Cocktail

Once the incisions healed, recovery finally ended, and he moved back into our apartment, Will began to work on his baby babble. He practiced trying to remember what it was like to be an infant until it became an obsession.

Will says he can remember when his language, the biological instinct, was pure and untainted by his parents' external influence. They brought with them into that little house in Palmetto Beach the semiotics of culture. He says if he concentrates hard enough he can put himself back into that mindset. He recites some of the baby babble and acts out some of the base responses to stimuli and environment, but then he says the stimuli and environment pour those cultural influences right back into his mind and he returns to, as he calls it, the wet sponge state.

Besides that, Will started to try out stand-up comedy, went to a couple open mic nights. The doctors had told him to get out there and do things anyway—public things. "Get out there," they said. So Will started doing it for his health, but soon it became his passion.

I went to every set; I remember every line. All of his sets were an amalgamation of classic standup tropes. Except on the Night of Sleepy Whispers—that was the night when everything changed, when we promised each other that we would stop eating takeout. This wasn't the only thing that changed, but it was pretty frustrating. We saved money, but it still sucked.

Will had only been drinking ginger ales that evening, which was weird for him. An obscure brand of tequila called Arco Iris was not only being kept in business because of him, but was thriving. The stuff tasted awful. I never understood why he likes it so much. It's not cheap and not easy to find.

Will tripped over his own feet as he walked across the stage of The Improv to the microphone. His hair was scraggly—it was always scraggly, but during his sets it was more scraggly than usual, and he had a tough time keeping the thin, greasy strands out of his eyes—and his clothes were (always) dirty and torn. It looked like a disgruntled dishwasher had glued all of their dirty rags to Will's body, a modern tar and feathering. The audience shook with anticipation. It was audible, a low hum: the vibrating of thirty or so slightly nervous bodies all ready to like Will, to laugh. The question on my mind every night during the standup days was, "Will Will show the audience that he likes them too?"

"You ever walk around in public," Will said, "start hearing a person talk, and think, 'Why the fuck do they talk like that? Oh right, because there's people who are different from me.'

See, this is why I don't leave the house. I'm out here walking around and there's other people in my way. What are you doing? This is where I walk."

The audience howled and the seal was broken.

After that, he screamed gibberish at the audience for half an hour. With Will's sets, it was more about the rhythm and the beats of his delivery than the material. It was like experimental music. After he finished, Will invited the members of the audience back to his apartment for dinner. They agreed, all of them except one. He had slipped into The Improv on accident but didn't want to be rude, so he sat through Will's performance. Outside, along the side of the building, waiting for Will to find his shoes, the audience chattered away about the Cooking Network show *I Eat, You Starve*; the guy apologized and excused himself, saying he needed to find out which theater was hosting his daughter's recital.

During the walk to Will's, I bragged about his apartment. I told Susy, Doug, Tammy, and everybody else all about how Will rented out a basement apartment underneath an abandoned factory. The candy that had been manufactured there was a short-lived brand called Tullie's. They were powdery green sugar cylinders that had been tainted with something hallucinogenic. They looked like the radioactive cylinder in the opening sequence of *The Simpsons*.

When we got to Will's place, we gathered in his living room. It was awkward at first, being crammed in so close to each other, but we suddenly forgot about the sardine discomfort when Will started chugging a bottle of Arco Iris. At first, I thought his invitation to witness the alcohol poisoning was supposed to be the finale of his routine. Everyone else seemed to think that, too; we were all muttering like a bunch of legless chickens. Will chugged another bottle of tequila and finally passed out. We clapped, shouted useless encore at him; somebody even threw roses on top of his nearly-dead body.

Then Will stood up and started cooking. His eyes were closed, but he was up and fiddling with the stove. We were all a little on edge at first, witnessing a sleepwalker sleepcooking; it was my first time seeing either happen. I grabbed the fire extinguisher and held it at the ready. As I held it, I read the inspection tag; this extinguisher was expired.

"That makes sense," I said.

"What?" Tammy said.

I shoved it back under the sink and prayed for safety.

Will kept at it and whipped up vegan mushroom satay for everyone. No kidding: it was better than tasty. This food Will had sleepcooked was scrumptious. It could've come from a five-star restaurant, not that I was an authority on tasty food. I had only been to two five-star restaurants in my life; the first time was for my dad's fiftieth birthday and the second time was after my granddad's death. It felt weird to go out and eat nice food after Richard had been eaten by cancer. We should've stayed in, had cold canned soup or something.

The audience sat and talked about the food for a while and then left, more than satisfied. I was so surprised by Will's cooking talent I chugged his last bottle of Arco Iris and passed out in his living room.

CHAPTER TWO
Replacement Parts

The next morning, Will slapped me awake and told me to get the fuck out of his cock-sucking apartment—his words.

"Why didn't you tell me you were a great cook?" I asked him as he punched me in the balls.

"I'm no cook," Will said, and punched me again.

I told him to stop punching my groin. "All this time I could have been mooching tasty grub off you."

"I'm no cook. Drop it."

"Make me tofu eggs benedict," I demanded.

"What did you call me?"

There was a knock on the door and Will answered. It was the audience, all of them huddled in front of the door like a hungry, confused monster movie mob without the torches and pitchforks. Greg lit a cigarette, so there was fire but no torches. All of them pulled forks out of their pockets—so no pitchforks—and licked their lips. They didn't all lick their lips at the same time; that would've been creepy, though the intermittent lip-licking was pretty creepy too, like the monster movie mob had morphed into a lounge of lizards.

Is a lounge of lizards named after lounge lizards—those Frank Sinatra fan people? Or are lounge lizards named after a lounge of lizards?

"Look," Will said. "If you want a refund for last night, take it up with The Improv."

"Please make us another dish, sir," Tex said.

Will turned and looked at me. His eyes looked like sad hound dog eyes. I broke eye contact and looked at my shoes. They were in bad shape; they looked more like mollusk shells. I figured I was still hammered.

"What is this?" Will asked me. "You're really starting to hurt my feelings."

"I'll pay a hundred dollars for whatever dish you make," Susy said. "All of us will." All of them nodded in agreement at the same time, which was somehow more creepy than the intermittent lip-licking.

Will turned back to the crowd. A customer service smile stretched across his face.

"Come right in," he said. "Have a seat wherever you'd like." He tried to take Tex's coat, but ended up ripping off his shirt, exposing bare torso. Tex didn't seem to mind. At one point he started flexing his pecs at everybody.

Will tried to make tofu eggs benedict. He really tried, but nothing happened. He brought out their plates, but there was nothing on them.

The audience left and did not pay. As he closed the door, Will scratched his head and looked at me. I shrugged at him.

"What happened?" he asked.

"You chugged two handles of Arco Iris, passed out, and cooked the best meal I or any of those weirdos have ever had."

"Well shit," Will said and ran for the front door. "Let's invite them to come back tonight." He looked like a dog excited for a walk. I half-expected him to pick up a leash with his teeth and whip it at me.

That night, Will chugged two more handles and passed out, again, in front of his now nicely-dressed guests. I caught eyes with Susy. She looked a lot like my mom. For some reason, I thought it would be a clever idea to go over and tell her this. Susy laughed in my face and most of the other audience members laughed at me.

"Are you my mother?" she said with a squeaky voice. I think she was referencing the children's book *Are You My Mother*?

As we patiently waited for Will to turn into a zombie chef, I thought about how peculiar the human experience can be. I thought about how odd it was to watch all these people standing around, waiting for a grown man to nearly kill himself with a poisonous liquid and then get up in his sleep to cook them fancy dishes. Also, I couldn't figure out where all of these ingredients were coming from.

In most cases, the marginalized are at least somewhat aware of their marginalization. Will was aware, but only when he wasn't being exploited and subcategorized. I guess he asked for it—maybe it was wishful thinking come to fruition on his part, like Hungry Hungry Hippos on chaos magick—but he did need to live. I think if he wasn't about to be kicked out of Candy Factory he would've shooed all these foodies away. Either way, one of us was going to be blamed for this.

Will's chateaubriand seitan was a hit though. Susy and Tex were so happy with the meal that they vigorously applauded. It was weird; they wouldn't stop, like they were caught in a loop of themselves eating thick potato chips into a loudspeaker. I stared at them a little too long and a little too judgmentally. Susy and Tex caught me looking, stopped applauding, and frowned.

Susy flared her nostrils at me. "Can somebody please turn on the air conditioner?"

I thought she was ripping on me, pointing out that the room was off balance because of how cold I was being and how emotionally warm her side of the apartment was. I chewed on this thought and the last bite of my seitan for a little while, not breaking eye contact with her. Without looking, I could tell that everyone else in the room felt uncomfortable.

But then I noticed that she was actually sweating, so I went to turn the air conditioner on.

Will never turns his air conditioner on. Whenever I bring up the modern miracle of air conditioning, he responds by telling me about sweating and evolution. His speeches are usually priggish, but his sweating and evolution speeches are especially infuriating. Tell me about that if I complain about sweating during a jog.

The heat of his apartment caused his refrigerator to overwork and eventually break, spoiling all of the food that Will never had in his old fridge. He called me over to help him turn the broken fridge into an art project. When I got there, he didn't answer the door. He was sitting on the couch looking through a shoebox of old photos.

"Hello," I said and waved a hand in front of his face. "The hell are you doing?"

Without looking away from the photos as he shuffled through them he said, "Looking for pictures of the kitchen. I figured I've snapped a few during a New Year's party or something."

"Are we still turning the fridge into a bobsled?"

He still wasn't paying attention to me, so I went into the kitchen. In a doorway behind where the old fridge had sat for years was a new fridge. Technically, the new fridge was an old fridge: a vintage lime green streamline refrigerator.

"Who the fuck put this food in here?" I asked Will. The fridge was filled with jackfruit and avocados, so I guessed the fridge was telling him to make pan-seared faux salmon with avocado remoulade. That abnormally cold summer night, that's what he made.

I noticed that night that the apartment was a lot more sardine-packed than the previous two nights. Each audience member had brought a guest along. Each guest was wide-eyed during the sleepcooking, watching, absorbing, analyzing, occasionally looking back at the friend who had invited them, probably convinced that an orgy was going to bust out at any moment. They kept looking back at their friend to silently ask, "Now?"

The audience gave him a standing ovation, but they were already standing so I don't know if it actually counts as a standing ovation.

Will and I realized a few days later that Will's refrigerator was not only producing ingredients for his meals, but that the thing could think. Under the ingredients list on the nutrition labels of some jars of vegan mayo were lines of words that looked pieced together like language, language that did not come from the label designers over at Joy!! Vegan Mayo. It took us way longer than it should've to figure out that these chunks of words were sentences.

Fridge expressed its concerns about Will's financial trouble. Fridge talked about Will's impending eviction. Fridge also talked about how it had feelings for Will. It told us that it knew it was a refrigerator, and that its talking about having a crush on someone could be taken as a threat or, at the very least, a bad refrigerator joke. So, Fridge clarified and said that it was infatuated with Will. I'm not sure why it felt the need to type all of that out rather than using the word 'infatuated' in the first place. I guess it was trying to show us its humanity.

Will never said that Fridge's infatuation turned him on, but he never said that it didn't turn him on.

CHAPTER THREE
The Big Move

Will learned the hard way that people named Colleen Conners don't like to be called Denise Richards. It doesn't matter if you've mistaken a dream for reality; they still don't like it. I don't know if all people named Colleen Conners don't like to be called Denise Richards, though. There's probably a few hundred who are indifferent, and three who enjoy it.

Will also learned that, like a giraffe, he couldn't just strain his neck trying to reach for an apple with his teeth and adapt to his surroundings, giving himself a longer neck by sheer willpower. Evolution doesn't work that way. The neck thing is another story.

During the burgeoning phase of his restau-
rateuring, when Will and I started implement-
ing Leftover Noondays—we would repurpose
half-eaten hunks of seitan and saliva-covered
sides into more money; we called them "leftovers with a purpose"—Will noticed one day
that a person allegedly named Denise Richards,
standing in his living room eating her meal with
the rest of the sardines, had a few wet spots on
her shirt, a shirt that was covered in a repeating
design of Frank Capra's head.

Will tore the corner off of one of our newly
printed menus, wrote HOBO SHOWER? on it, and
and slid the note across his coffee table at her,
wildly smirking as he tried to make eye contact. As he leaned into the note-slide, not paying attention to his surroundings, he fell onto
the mahogany table, knocking her red wine off
the table and onto her knees, ruining her jeans.

She didn't slap him because of the content
of the note. She didn't even read the note; it had
been destroyed by the wine, rendered a moist,

red pile of meaninglessness. The arrangement of words meant, "Did you recently take a shower in the style of a houseless person?" meaning washing oneself off in a sink, usually in a public restroom. Further context: the note did not intend to disparage her or the houseless.

Over the last few Leftover Noondays, Will had gotten to know Denise Richards and he told her all about how, if he decides last-minute to go to the beach bar, Gravy Clementine's, right after work to visit someone named Weather, he normally takes a hobo shower, either at work or in the bathroom of the Fort Desoto State Park on his way to Treasure Island—the resort island in Pinellas County, not the book by Robert Louis Stevenson. He told Denise that he normally ends up with wet spots all over his clothes since he never has a towel handy. I suspected that Weather was not this person's real name, if she were even real. I think Will called her that because, as he described her, "She's always changing."

Will figured Denise Richards would've found the note funny, but she only noticed the ruining of her pants. Will later told me that he realized he hadn't been getting to know Denise Richards. He wasn't even sure if that was her name. He only dreamt that he had told her all of those things about the shower.

Will is proficient in the language of gibberish; had she read the note, she wouldn't have even batted an eye at the absurdity. She probably would've read the note, put it back down on the table, taken a conservative sip of her wine, and continued her conversation about *I Eat, You Starve* with Tex.

The person whose name we found out wasn't Denise Richards, but was Colleen Conners, threatened to shut Will's operation down. Will apologized and told her that he would pay for the jeans. He told me a few days later that he had the urge to explain to Colleen all about the note, the dream, and the shower, but he decided against it because, in the dream, I kept telling him to quit while he was ahead. I told him in real life to stop listening to dream versions of myself, even though my dream version self sounded sensible just like real life me. So I told him to stop dreaming all together.

What Will and I could agree on, though, was that we needed a bigger space for the restaurant. So, we broke into the ground floor of Candy Factory and made some assessments. Tables: we definitely needed tables, and lots of them. Chairs, too; people would finally stop complaining about having to stand. They would also, hopefully, stop sweating as much. There was no carpet up here—the floor was a beautiful terrazzo—but, still, we were tired of our customers sweating everywhere.

If Will could just forget what he dreamt about, we'd be golden, but he kept remembering his dreams. And as far as temperature goes, it wasn't cool up here. It was hot as hell. Either way, with all the extra room up here we could practice spin kicks.

A day into the renovations and we had noticed all kinds of quirks. We kept getting whiffs of a funny-smelling gas, but after laughing for a long time we would forget all about it. Some of the bricks in the wall of the factory would talk to me and say some messed up stuff, stuff I don't feel comfortable repeating. We also kept hearing voices coming from the hole in the floor we came up through over on the east end of the factory floor. At first, we thought squatters had already claimed Will's apartment, but when we climbed down there we couldn't find anybody. I had my suspicions about the quirks being hallucinations caused by that gas we kept forgetting about, but Will would tell me not to bring up the gas. He would also periodically scream about not pulling him into my web of lies.

"Don't you dare besmirch the name of my precious gas," Will reminded me while I helped him unload the chairs and tables we'd stolen from an estate sale.

"You don't even know the name of that gas," I told him as I pulled my back.

I guess that's what happens when one is alive or stays in the same place for a long time: you notice weird shit. Old guys jiggling salt and pepper shakers always look patriarchal, probably always are patriarchal. The furious shaking of tiny cylinders—if it's Thanksgiving, little bloodthirsty pilgrims—appears oppressive.

Salt and pepper shakers were the last items we needed, and Will finally picked out a set an hour before grand opening. Will wasn't picky when we stole the chairs and tables, or any of the other crap. I don't understand why he was so damn picky with the shakers. I guess it was because they were the only items he ended up spending money on. He had tried a couple truck runs—we were sure the Pier Thirty and Sears trucks would have salt and pepper shakers on them—but, to Will's violent frustration, the hits were unsuccessful.

We were really starting to settle into a happy little rut. Candy Factory's ground floor truly looked like it would work as a restaurant. Will and I moved the kitchen upstairs into the old factory manager's office, a suspended box fastened to the side of the upper wall, held up with steel stilts and looking out over the factory floor. Leading from the floor to the office door was a wrought iron staircase, ornately designed with snarling dachshunds.

The sunlight coming in through the tilted ceiling windows made the factory look like an old train station. Will and I looked out over the restaurant from the top of the stairs. I was feeling pretty accomplished, but then Will told me to get my melon head out of the clouds.

"You haven't done a thing," Will said, "except exploit me and mooch."

I told Will that I thought it was neat that Candy Factory looked like a train station, but not like the train station from that Prince music video. It would be weird if Candy Factory looked like that. I remembered the late eighties and early nineties, when interior decorations looked like that video.

CHAPTER FOUR
Every Lemon Wedge
Costs a Dollar

Fridge didn't take Will's wine spilling, the heat, or the general move upstairs well. It started giving us spoiled meat. Will and I kept telling ourselves about how this was the nature of the restaurant business. Starting out is always shaky, no matter how well you try to balance and level off with meticulous planning, but we had never planned anything in our lives, meticulously or otherwise. We were just talking out of our asses.

While the customers couldn't have been happier with the bigger space, the spoiled food was not only making them mad, but sick, too. On opening night, Will vanished and left me to rely on utilizing our quickly dwindling leftovers supply. I tried my hand at sleepcooking a couple times, but every time I chugged two bottles of Arco Iris I woke up in the hospital. Susy kept finding me under Will's desk with my hands sticking out and stuffed into the bottom drawers. Will had stolen the desk from the office of the locally famous private investigator, Kentucky Jones. Will's plan was to make the kitchen look like a cross between a kitchen and a 1930s private investigator's office. Kentucky Jones wasn't from the 1930s—he was alive and well, and younger, too: in his late thirties—but his aesthetic was 1930s private investigator.

I tried different liquors a couple times: gin first, then vodka. I also woke up in the hospital those times. I tried mixing whiskey and sake once. That time I woke up in a bathtub full of ice. I was missing my appendix. Apparently, it was about to burst.

By the time we ran out of leftovers and I finally stopped almost killing myself with alcohol, Will had begun what would turn out to be his month-long sabbatical at Treasure Island—still not the book, just Will's old stomping grounds. So I even tried out regular cooking. I figured that I could be okay at it as long as I followed a recipe and didn't chug two bottles of tequila.

Customers noticed right away that Will wasn't doing the cooking. Peanut butter sandwiches with jelly on the side and grilled cheese sandwiches minus the cheese gave it away. That, and customers liked to come up the stairs and press their faces against the office window. They could clearly see that it was me regular cooking and not Will sleepcooking.

I guess I wasn't very good at cooking, even with the recipe following. Also, I still couldn't get any food that wasn't spoiled out of Fridge. I begged and pleaded with Fridge, but it gave no response. That's when it hit me—the refrigerator door hit me in the head when I bashed my head into it during a fit of rage—and I realized that Will and I never once made it a point to find out personal details about Fridge. I asked Fridge for its name. I asked where it was manufactured, if it had parents and siblings, if it ever lived anywhere else. I apologized for Will's behavior and I apologized for moving upstairs without asking. I remembered the messages it sent us on the food packages, so I wrote my questions on the back of a receipt I found in the wallet of the truck driver from the last hit and left the note in the crisper drawer.

An hour later, Fridge left a twelve page note on the packages of asparagus. Fridge told me its name was Refrigerator, or Fridge for short. Fridge explained to me why there's an added 'd' in the shortened version of the word 'Refrigerator.' It also told me that I was a dummy for asking any of these questions. It said it never lived anywhere else, unless the time it spent in the loading facility waiting to be shipped to Candy Factory counted. It had only ever lived in that basement and it said it was pretty pissed about the move upstairs. Fridge told me it was almost ready to forgive Will, but not quite. It still had strong feelings for Will. Fridge told me that it knew that kind of thing could never work out between them. It wasn't even sure where these feelings came from and why it could suddenly think and rationalize. It just woke up one day a couple months ago and was able to think and rationalize. It blamed the toxicity of Tampa's water and so did I.

"I agree," I said, as I wrote my agreement on another receipt. It felt trippy and coincidental to be in agreement with a fridge, but I told myself it was just my mind using the portion of my brain that processes memory in a serpentine, roundabout way.

The trippiest parts of a trip are always the coincidences.

"Why are you slipping a receipt into the crisper drawer of that refrigerator?" Ruby Gerry asked me. He was standing behind me next to Will's desk, staring at me with his dead eyes.

Ruby's eyes aren't dead in a penetrating, creepy way. They're dead in a boring way, like he's always thinking about his favorite brand of peanut butter crackers. Ruby used to make commercials for Sound Exchange, and he would show up at FuBar whenever Will and I decided to spend an evening getting FUBAR'd. Every time, no matter what, we always saw Ruby. Every time they told me I had a visitor, I'd walk all the way to the visitation hall, and there he was in all of his boring peanut butter cracker glory. When Ruby wasn't being boring he was talking smack about Tampa's water supply, about its supposed toxicity, which is still pretty boring.

"The refrigerator is alive, and its name is Refrigerator," I told him as he pulled a packet of peanut butter crackers out of his breast pocket. "Fridge for short."

"I told you about Tampa's water supply," Ruby said and took a nibble. "Didn't I?" He went on to tell me that Will was out of control, that he'd stolen all of the original audience and brought them across the bridge to Gravy's. He was performing standup for them and encouraging them to spend all of their money on greasy bar food.

"I didn't even know Gravy's had a kitchen." I looked out at the dining room and saw that this was true. All thirty of the original thirty were gone. In fact, the restaurant was mostly empty. I thought the food I was making was decent, but everyone had figured out that it wasn't Will sleepcooking the decent food.

While Ruby told me all about Will, I opened Fridge and pulled out a bundle of Cuban bread. Floridians are weird: we keep our bread in the refrigerator especially during the summer when it's humid. This doesn't make sense, because while it's true that moisture is what causes bread to go stale, putting the bread in the fridge speeds up the crystallization of starches.

I ate the bread in front of Ruby and he

vomited a little. Ruby isn't a huge fan of bread. He says the image of it sitting in stomach acid flashes in his mind whenever he watches someone eat it.

Ruby wiped his face and started talking shit about Tampa's water. I shuffled some of the papers on Will's desk, trying to drown out the sound of Ruby's voice. He wouldn't shut up, so I told him about how the water was probably what brought Refrigerator to life—that or Will's precious gas. Ruby asked if Fridge materializes food out of thin air or if it teleports already existing food. We talked about how if Fridge materializes the food out of thin air, we could solve world hunger. We knew we probably wouldn't because no one in the history of humanity who has had the ability to solve world hunger has done it. The second option scared us; we didn't want to steal food from anyone.

"Tampa's water," I said to Ruby, "is probably what caused Will to go AWOL."

"There isn't a doubt in my mind," Ruby said.

"That or his precious gas."

"Look at what lead in the air did to people from the twenties to the eighties."

"How have his sets been?"

"Brilliant."

I've always had trouble utilizing humor. One time, while driving with Will and Ruby through St. Petersburg—Florida, not Russia— I told them that I wished the driver's seat was an ejector seat, so I could watch Ruby fly out of the Ford Focus. Ruby took it to mean that I wanted him to get the fuck out of the car. What I meant was that I wanted to watch an absurd thing happen. In retrospect, I can see why the ejector seat comment could be taken as a fuck-you.

Rube gave me a ride to Treasure Island— which by now you'd think I wouldn't have to differentiate from the book by Robert Louis Stevenson. We found the beach bar Will was always hanging out at, Gravy Clementine's. He wasn't there. Weather wasn't there either.

Gravy's was super Floridian: one big patio with a tiki bar in the center, every open space covered with thatched palm frond roof. I could imagine how romantic it was during the rainy season, tiny amounts of rain slipping through the spaces of the leaf roof and dripping intermittently all over the day-drunks.

"Hey," I said to the bartender. "Is Weather working tonight?"

"Get lost," the bartender told me.

"Doesn't that just happen organically?" I said, and began to hate myself.

"Quit being a wise ass and get lost," he said.

"Okay," I said and continued to not move, staring at him like a creep.

"Fuck off."

So I did. Rube and I headed for the exit when I noticed the original thirty. The bartender caught up to us, panting.

"You *can* purposefully get lost," he said. "Put on a blindfold, get drunk, and take a long walk in some forest you are unfamiliar with, in any order."

"Don't get smart with my friend here," Ruby said. I guess he was defending my honor. "He'll ruin you."

I told Ruby, "Don't put words in my mouth."

I decided that it would be best if I removed myself from this conversation and radius of soon-to-be-swinging-fists. I walked up to Terry and Jacob, and awkwardly inserted myself into their heated examination of a recent Will set.

"What do you think he meant," Terry asked Jacob, "when he said, 'I miss Grover Cleveland'?" Terry's horn-rimmed glasses made him look much more sophisticated than he probably was, although that was probably just me feeling bad about myself. His burnt-orange coat was super cool though. I really did think it looked dashing on him.

"Maybe," Jacob replied, "he wished we still had classically conservative Democrats." Jacob's oversized houndstooth coat reminded me of the time Will and I lifted six thousand dollars' worth of houndstooth fabric from Jo-Ann Fabrics. My hands went itchy as I considered stealing the coat.

"I doubt it's that simple," Terry said.

"I hear that," I said. A few yards behind me, back at the exit, the bartender was kicking Ruby's ass.

"The fuck are you doing here?" Jacob asked me and shook a fist at me, very close to my nose. Terry asked the same thing, only Terry shook a foot at me, very close to my crotch.

The bartender finished kicking his ass, grabbed Ruby by his hair, and smashed Ruby's face into the concrete patio wall.

"I'm just looking for Will," I said. "Please don't hurt me."

Ruby snuck into the conversation, rushing, holding both of his eyes. I thought he had grown a third arm (maybe some condition brought on by Tampa's water) because there was a third hand holding his bloody nose. Then, I realized that the bartender was holding it for him.

"Goober Squeezeland," Rube said with a squeak.

"Your friend is probably concussed," the bartender said. "You should take him to the hospital."

"That's where I was born," Ruby said directly to Terry, really close to Terry's face.

"Congratulations," Terry said. "Now get out of my face."

"Will is with Weather," Jacob said.

"Is that their real name: Weather?" I asked.

"Yes," Jacob and Terry said simultaneously, which was easily as as creepy as their and everyone else's intermittent lip-licking the night after Will first sleepcooked.

I told them that we missed them over at Candy Factory. They corrected me and told me that I missed their money. I overcompensated and promised them live entertainment if they returned to us, and this made me feel dirty. Terry adjusted his horn-rimmed glasses and snickered at me.

I shuffled away and walked around Gravy Clementine's, bugging the rest of the originals. I didn't plant spying devices on them; I just bothered them with questions about Will. Terry and Jacob mingled, zig-zagging around my path, pointing out how pathetic I was to the other random day-drunk guests.

I asked the originals if they knew where Will and Weather were and if they at least knew when Will and Weather would return. I asked if Will sleepcooked here. Most of the originals shrugged me off and acted like tight-lipped mobsters. Still, I thought they were all pretty cool. They'd always been cool, but now they were especially cool. Maybe it was the amount of ice in their drinks. All of them hunched when they responded to my questions from their seats. The dim lighting of Gravy's patio was doing the atmosphere favors, too, affecting everyone, not only making them look cool, but feel cool. I think I was possibly cool too. It was like a scene out of *Casablanca*.

I turned around to find Ruby. I wanted to walk down the beach with him for a little while and admire the full moon, and dunk his head in the salt water. I wanted to see if that would help his alleged concussion. Concussions don't work that way, but I figured I'd give it a shot.

The bartender, I found out later, took Ruby to the emergency room after realizing that I had no intention of helping him.

CHAPTER FIVE
Don't Test Me

I don't come to Pinellas County often, but every time I do I feel better. Maybe it's the beach. Living by the beach has got to make a populace a few mimosas happier. And look, I love my hometown—I don't wake up and go to sleep in St. Pete every day—so maybe I just have a case of over-saturation, but Tampa feels so angry all the time. Especially Ybor. Sometimes I think the Church of Scientology out there is sending their people down 7th and 8th Ave. to stalk the residents, to systematically make people feel worthless and paranoid. Ybor City is the perfect place to do that. The place is one big bar. I wondered if Sarasota is like Tampa; they have a Scientology headquarters down there. It might be the HQ.

I walked down the beach, soaking up the moonlight, and remembered a dream I had many years ago: Muzak was blaring from the stereo system of the Scientology building. Everyone started puking. The heads of the Church clambered out of their offices and began slurping up the puke, chunky, soupy gulp by chunky, soupy gulp. The business was giving us the business, if you know what I mean. Somebody must have been trying to scare somebody with all that Muzak into buying a shitload of Lockheed Martin merchandise. I knew this tactic. I wanted to believe in the stalking and thinly veiled lies. They've been known to use psychological warfare on the inside, so why not outside? It's not like governments and corporations haven't been using psychological warfare for, well, forever. A greedy few have always prospered through the suffering of others. It's almost like the civil part of civilization is the thinly veiled lie.

I have these stupid notions all the time, but I keep thinking they're at least halfway decent shower thoughts.

After that little conversation with myself, I decided to dunk my head in the water, told myself I deserved a little punishment for all of my hogwash, but then realized that the water felt refreshing. I dunked myself a couple more times for fun.

"I'm not a witch!" I screamed every time I pulled myself out of the water, doubling down on the self-punishment. "I'm not a witch!"

"Poor things," an old, bearded, overweight man who looked a lot like Santa Claus said. He was behind me on the shore, letting the tide roll back and forth over his bare feet. I thought that he was even wearing the Santa suit, but as Gulf water dripped out of my eyes I saw that he was wearing red sweatpants and a red hoodie.

"What?" I yelled to him over the crashing

waves. I stepped out of the Gulf of Mexico, seaweed draped across my clothes. I felt very fashion-forward.

"Poor things," he said. "The little ones. They were so thirsty."

"Yes," I said. "May their houses smell like Douglas Fir all year round and may their chimneys always be easy to climb down."

"Did you not hear about the water?"

Santa—not the real Santa; his name was George, but I wanted to call him Santa— invited me up the beach into the recreation room of the motel after I started speaking in tongues. It was like a Florida sunroom, except it was filled with rec room stuff, plus a gross old couch and a tiny bar. It was more like a Midwestern basement rumpus room, except always swelteringly hot. Although, I suppose a rumpus room from the 1970s probably got pretty hot with all those uncles and leisure suits. I hadn't actually been speaking in tongues; I bit my tongue after he gave me the news about the water: how there had been some kind of spill in the gulf, how it'd gotten into the pipes and pools. Children were tripping balls, their tongues turned green like glowworms. My first inclination was to call bullshit, but I told myself to bite my tongue until he had explained everything. No one tells you how easy it is to do, or how much blood there'll be.

Santa sat me down at the tabletop *The Simpsons* arcade machine and went into another room somewhere.

Remember that game? A jewel heist goes wrong and Maggie ends up kidnapped.

Eventually he returned with a steaming mug and a pot. He ripped the seaweed off of me, set the weeds in the pot, wrapped a sandy blanket around me, handed me the mug filled with cocoa, and set a red plastic cup filled with quarters on the table. The recreation room was disturbing; it was the foosball table and billiards table that made the rec room feel uneasy. I'm still not sure why those tables, specifically, affect me like this. I'm not even sure if this is the sole reason that the recreation room was disturbing.

"You'll get all of this figured out," Santa said to me and left, pot in hand. It all felt very libertarian.

So I played the arcade game all night. I won level after level, quarter after quarter, and fell in love with the rec room. The foosball and billiards tables didn't look like they wanted to eat me anymore. I vowed to one day build myself a rec room just like this one.

As the sun rose, I watched an actual swarm of locusts swarm the beach from the window behind the arcade machine. The room smelled like my feet, the red plastic cup was empty, and my stomach was also empty.

Right before I got up to complain, Santa came in with a cup of coffee for me.

"Santa," I said, staring out the window at the crazy number of locusts. "It's fake, right? It's like a dog wagging, like that movie *Wag the Dog*, right?"

"Stop calling me Santa," Santa said. "My name is George. That's what my wonderful mother named me, so I would appreciate it if you called me George."

"I want to live here, Santa," I said. "Mornings here are gorgeous."

"That's it," Santa said. "Get out."

I have never met a person younger than seventy whom I couldn't talk with about The Simpsons for at least an hour. If they're over seventy I can get in at least a half- hour. *The Simpsons* crosses divisions in our society. Next election, the candidates should shoot the shit about *The Simpsons* for an hour before tackling any of the issues. Next time, I told myself, I would talk about The Simpsons with Santa before attempting to negotiate a lease.

As I exited the recreation room down to the beach, Will bumped into me on the path between the tiny dunes. He was carrying a towel and was wearing a red bathing suit and red flip flops. I was jealous of his outfit.

"What the hell are you doing here?" Will asked me.

"I was looking for you at Gravy's. Ruby got a concussion and the bartender who concussed him took him to the hospital. I went for a midnight stroll on the beach. A man who looked like Santa Claus let me play his Simpsons arcade game in a motel rec room until he kicked me out for calling him Santa. It's a cool bar, by the way—Gravy's."

"Well, you were just calling 'em like you see 'em," Will said. "There's nothing wrong with that."

"Somebody is trying to sell me something," I said. "I can never remember what, though."

"When you're right," Will said with a serious face post-ironically stretched across the front of his head.

"So, you're staying?"

"Gulf air is good for the skin."

I couldn't blame him. I had never seen him so happy. I didn't want to ask about what we should do with Candy Factory or Fridge. I didn't ask him if he was coming back.

I felt a tap on my shoulder. I thought I was about to be assassinated, but assassins usually don't tap your shoulder right before they do the deed, unless they like to briefly taunt their victims first.

"Yikes," Will said at the sight of Ruby's fucked-up face.

"Thanks for your concern last night," Ruby said to me. He turned his attention to Will. "Party's over. Time to get back to work." Ruby set a satisfied hand on his hip.

"Fuck you, Rube," Will said. "You have zero association with Candy Factory." Will pointed to me. "And don't you tell me what to do either, you soda can missing its stay-tab."

"Learn to improvise and open me with a butter knife," Ruby said.

"Shut up Rube," Will said.

"Yeah, shut up Rube," I said, parroting Will.

"They sure are big shoes to fill," Rube said to me.

* * * * *

"Everything or nothing, and not a smidge of anything between as deemed by everyone but the individual, time shifts and changes all modern hearts. Tragedy on a grand scale is always the shifter. I just wonder: when did it happen? Where is the nodal point? This shift probably happened in the seventies or something."

That's a line from one of Will's sets; it came from a conversation we used to have every Friday at FuBar. Will's stress level would elevate tenfold during this conversation; he used to drink coffee with his booze. After years of constantly clenching his jaw, he cracked a molar. Will called the injury The Shattered Tension Occurrence, and whenever he's not quite blackout drunk he says something like, "It's the nodal point of my undoing."

Will finally got that cracked tooth extracted not too long ago. A few tiny chunks were left behind in his gums and he had to go back to the dentist to have them removed. The dentist told him the little chunks could have gone up into his head and killed him. I have adopted this story as my personal allegory for life. I tell it to everyone I see whenever I'm drunk.

I told my Dad this story once and he told me to stop clenching my jaw. I give my parents slack. Lead wasn't completely phased out of gasoline until 1995.

Ruby asked Will if he liked his hair and Will said no and then yes. I asked Will if he had a set tonight at Gravy's and he told he me had one every night and that I wasn't particularly welcome but that it was a free country, so if I wanted to watch his set that would be fine, that I probably wouldn't get on his nerves too much. The locusts had been scuttling our way since Will and I first bumped into each other, and our bodies were now covered in them.

"Fridge misses you," I told him.

Will ignored me. "I wish everything that smelled good was edible." He picked a plump locust off his hand and ate it.

Have you ever had trouble seeing after going outside for the first time in weeks? I don't mean that in an esoteric way. I can't stand the August heat. I stay inside for most of the month and when September begins I go outside. My eyes take a long time to adjust. Everything is just a bit blurry for a while.

We went to Gravy Clementine's. Rube drove and wouldn't shut the hell up.

He kept saying things like:

"My knees always itch."

"Do you guys ever get chest pains?"

And, "God, it's hard to see out here. It's that weird diffused cloud cover light. What's going on with you guys? You're not squinting at all. That cloud over there is pissing me off."

Will asked me, "When was the last time you saw Skibs?"

Skibs McGong is my oldest friend. I met him in the seventh grade during the first day of third period P.E. The teacher, Ms. Weaver, told us kids that we could either play the sport of the day or walk laps. I usually walked laps, so I started walking and Skibs did too. We started talking. We didn't stop talking for a long time. We're still talking; even if it's been years, we pick the conversation right back up, like a much less intelligent version of that twenty-year conversation between Noam Chomsky and his colleague, Mr. What's-His-Name. He helped me disassemble my Dad's desk in the tenth grade, and when we finished my Dad was sobbing in the corner of the office.

"A couple years ago," I said, "during Horse Spill Fest."

"What the flying radish is a Horse Spill Fest?" Ruby asked, hands tightly clutching the steering wheel like he was considering killing us all by swerving into oncoming traffic.

"One day, Rube," Will said, in his comfortable position in the backseat, "I will kiss you."

"Okay," Ruby said, chuckled, shrugged, and loosened his grip on the steering wheel.

We arrived at Gravy's unscathed. I flung

open the passenger door and jumped out of the car. I landed pretty hard on my heel and it felt like it was going to bruise. Skibs jumped out of the Dodge parked next to us and scared the heel pain out of me.

"I wish the last episode of *Telemore* had more gunfights," I said to Skibs.

"Where would Susan have put these extra gunfights?" Skibs said. "She is a master writer-director. Don't you dare question her."

I'm always shaking hands with people well after it should be happening. If I were formally introduced to Harrison Ford and then we worked together—and assuming Harrison Ford liked me—he wouldn't expect to keep shaking hands every time we saw each other. We would show up for interviews and he'd expect the handshakes to be replaced with quiet jokes. And sometimes when I interact with old friends it feels like they know about a terminal illness that I'm unaware of, an illness slowly working its way through my squishy system, so they feel the need to oblige my hand-shaking and shower thoughts and tangents because they know I don't know I'm going to die. But I never feel this way with Skibs.

We left behind Will and Ruby and headed inside Gravy's, letting the soles of our shoes scrape across the gravel lot, not caring.

Will's set was wacky. I hate the word wacky, but that's what it was, though I didn't hate it. I didn't understand half of what he said, but it was like music. If Parliament and Pavement had a p-word baby band that was actually a standup set, Will would be the Papa.

After his set, Will joined our table and we shot the junk the rest of the night. It was loud out there on the patio, extra loud. I liked that. I'm extra excitable around Skibs and I tend to shout about what I'm excited about, and the loud atmosphere gave me an excuse to let loose. The last joint Skibs and I hung out at after Horse Spill was extra quiet: the kind of silence that hurts my ears, makes conversation stilted and uncomfortable, makes it feel like my words are way more important than they should be.

I'd told the bartender, "It's eerily quiet in here."

"Humans need silence. It's a fact."

"I came out to get away from silence. When most people go out, they are escaping silence."

"We have hot sauce pizza. It's not just our specialty; hot sauce pizza is a thing, far and wide across the land. Are you aware we invented it though?"

"I'll have some of that," I'd told him and smiled. We'd both known the subject needed to change.

Skibs screamed compliments and criticisms about Will's set, and Will laughed at this. I could tell that he was really enjoying himself and it made me happy. I know Will has a life of his own and enjoys himself all the time, but sometimes it's hard to imagine. I know Skibs and myself aren't the only thing that can make Will happy. I can be pretty concieted, but I'm not that concieted. It just makes me happy to see my friends happy.

"And you," Skibs said to me. "You are a terrible liar and a conspirator."

When I first discovered alcohol, I would pour it into a red plastic cup with Sprite and walk around my parent's neighborhood in the middle of the night. Their neighborhood was quiet and spooky all the time, like everyone was living in *Footloose*. I wore headphones and blasted Revolver. I didn't want to hurt anybody or anything like that. I just wanted to feel incredible. And whenever I dipped my toe in booze, a pool without a shallow end, and I fell in, I did.

I know some of the neighbors saw me stumbling down the street. They probably told my parents. Everybody thought I was nuts. I'm sure I looked scary to them, getting wasted down those quiet streets in the middle of the night. Everyone always use to tell me that I reminded them of Jeffery Dahmer. Now, any time

I meet someone I can't help but think that I remind them, too, of Jeff.

"Was that loud enough for you?" Colleen Conners said, looming over our table. I hadn't seen Colleen since the wine-spilling and note-slipping. The three of us asked her what she was talking about. She pointed at Will's Jucifer shirt. "Gazelle doesn't know it, but she's in love with me. I've been following their RV around the states this tour. Four cars back is the best distance on the interstate. Tabby has been following them for fifteen years. He doesn't even remember where he's originally from. He thinks like New England or something."

Colleen sat down with us and told us about her successful custom amplifier business.

"My bartender introduced me to her parents," Will told me.

Will, Skibs, Colleen, and I drank all night and into the morning on the patio. Some of the original thirty periodically pulled up a chair and hung out for a while, but all of them eventually turned in. Not us though. Not saying we're badasses for drinking all night and morning, just pointing out that maybe I had a drinking problem. I have no idea where Ruby went, but I didn't care, though I was a little worried that the bartender had concussed him again—so maybe I did care.

As the sun got pretty high up there, nearly noon-high, I began to worry about Fridge. I don't know why. It'd been doing fine all these years, though it hadn't been sentient that long. What would happen if the power went out? Would it die? I started to panic.

"You doing alright there buddy?" Skibs asked. " You're all flush like a scared tomato."

"Are you going to come back to your restaurant?" I asked Will.

Skibs laughed. "You run a restaurant?"

"Yeah," Will said. "Yeah to both of you. I'll be moseying back to Candy Factory soon."

"Candy Factory?" Skibs asked. "Your apartment?"

"We moved upstairs," I told Skibs. The

bartender brought the check and three mints.

"It looks like the train station from that Prince music video," Colleen said.

"Yeah," Will said. "I guess it kind of does."

The seagulls called to each other, probably us too. I know that's a vain thought, but I have a way with birds. I'm like a Disney princess. The hum of the Gulf waves, which had been out of mind all night and morning, suddenly pushed back into my mind as the man sitting in the bushes on the edge of the patio began singing a song about the hum of the Gulf waves. He stopped to take a swig of mouthwash and then started a new song, an unnerving one.

"Had himself some of that clickbait psychology," he sang, stopping to chug the mouthwash.

He continued: "Every smile was pseudo-psychology accrued and applied. Devious intention and mixing bowl logic. I open my car door and look at the ground. Clickbait psychology makes this mean something."

I shook my head at this. "You're either a nut

or you're not a nut in the hopscotching Bay."

"America is obsessed with binary opposition," Will said. "You're just succumbing."

What kind of nut was I even referring to? Almond, pecan, clinical? Or was I just calling him an asshole? I felt bad. The songbird could have just been a rascal.

"I'm drunk," I said to Will. We're all drunk."

"I'm not," Will said.

"Me neither," Skibs said.

The rascal in the bush stopped singing, finished off his mouthwash, and started singing again, this time about a vegan shepherd's pie recipe.

"Eat a table," I said. Will held up his hands, surrendering.

"You're acting like one of those people who get all bent out of shape when you say you don't like a certain movie or TV show or band," Will said.

"Yikes," Colleen said. She scooted her chair back and left, escaping the unsavory moment.

I was drunk and feeling dumber than usual. I was one of the assholes, so I slammed my fists on the table.

"Trash talk *Beetlejuice* all you want," I yelled. "My personality is not built around the media I consume."

Skibs lowered his head onto the table.

"Night night," he said.

The German word for feeling embarrassed for someone else is 'fremdschämen.'

"Any of you rascals want to buy some sentient pool equipment?" the asshole in the bush said to us. He was now out of the bush and standing over us.

It sounded like a good idea to me, but I was drunk, Skibs was asleep, and Will was politely declining.

"There's something in the water, isn't there?" I asked the asshole.

CHAPTER SIX
Fremdschämen

I followed the asshole, who I found out was
not, in fact, named Asshole but Jim, back to his
pool supply store, where he showed me around
and introduced me to each living pool supply.
That was when I met the pump. Jim wrote a
note on some loose paper and dumped it into
the intake. A few minutes later, it sprayed some
water onto the store floor. The puddle was in
the shape of a message. It read:

NICE TO MEET YOU. MY NAME IS PUMP,
BUT I PREFER PUMPY.

I could just feel the day turning into one of
those days.

"Did I overhear from my bush that you run
a failing restaurant?"

"Yeah," I said. "You did overhear that, asshole."

Before 'asshole' meant 'jerk,' it meant 'crazy,' and before that it meant 'butthole.'

"Add a pool to the business," Jim said.

I thought of Dockside Jack's in St. Clair Shores. They had a pool on their deck and I remember seeing drunk middle-aged boaters fuck in it when I was a kid. That was the Midwest, though, and this was Florida. I figured it would probably work. If not, I'd have a pool to swim around in when I was alone and not making money. So, I had the pool built and I bought Pumpy.

The money for all this was easy to come by. I found Will's photo album collection, filled with photos from the early 60s to the late 70s. I think they belonged to his parents at some point; one of the people featured in a lot of the pictures looked like a younger version of his mom. The albums felt like the music video for "Rocky Mountain High," and there was a market for stuff that felt like that. I sold Will's photo albums for forty-six thousand dollars.

I couldn't decide whether to build one inside next to the dining area or outside, so I had two pools built. I bought another pump, also named Pumpy, and built a patio out back around the pool. The indoor pool connected to the hole that lead down into Will's old apartment, so I set up scuba lessons with an instructor, Jen, on Wednesdays. Jen would take the students down into the apartment to search for Will's porn collection. The winner would get half-off on their dinner.

And guess what: the pool was a hit. After a while, no one seemed to even remember the sleepcooking gimmick. We had barbeque seitan and ten percent off the cheap liquor on Fridays, also known as Sloppy Seitan Fridays. We even got Susy and Tex to come back. Even Fridge was in exceptionally highs spirits. All of its messages were covered in hearts and smiley faces. Everybody was having a good time and I was feeling a little better about running Candy Factory. It's like my Dad always used to say: "Interactive gimmicks are better than sleep-cooking gimmicks." He didn't say that all the time, but he was alive for a long time and he talked a lot. That assemblage of words probably found its way out of his mouth.

I'm a sucker for documentaries. Stick me in front of any documentary and I'll be for or against whatever thing the movie is trying to make me for or against. Shove some cleverly juxtaposed images and a voice-over with some well-timed music cues together and you've hooked me. Also, in real life, if you say things to me with enough declarative verve I will believe anything you say. I'll feel like an expert on the subject too. God help me if you ask me anything about the subject after it's all said and done.

At some point, that celebrity chef from Smash Mouth showed up one day to film an episode of *I Eat, You Starve*. The whole thing was weird, kind of a downer. It wasn't like the rest of the show. For some reason, the Smash Mouth guy edited it together like a World War Two documentary, complete with grainy black and white footage and sad orchestral music.

The whole thing was super serious, and it made me look like Mussolini on the balcony. They kept cutting back to the same shot they got of me standing at the top of the stairs. I'm shouting and it's in slow motion, so I look angry, but I was only yelling with glee to the crowd that I had just sliced the cherry pie.

Despite the weird angle of that episode, people flocked to Candy Factory and I made too much money. I should've used the money, or at least the free food I was getting from Fridge, to help out the less fortunate. Looking back, I'm sure that if Fridge was aware of world affairs, it would've forced me to donate our profit and food to charity during the Loadsamoney Era of Candy Factory.

A few months into the new and improved Loadsamoney Era, I decided to have a Grand Reopening, one that would knock the whole town on its ass. I took out a full-page advertisement in the *Tampa Times* and the *St. Pete Times*. We used to have the *Tampa Tribune*, but they folded after the owner was arrested for murdering and eating seventy-three people. I wanted Fridge to see the ad, since she was the one who really ran the joint, so I slipped both Times into her crisper drawer.

I called Gravy's and asked if Will was around. I wanted to invite him to show what a success the Factory had become, and to give him his portion of the profits. The bartender said he'd check. He slammed the phone on a firm surface, probably the bar top, and the staticky smack crunched in my ear. He came back a half hour later and told me to stop calling. It was better that way; Will would've shown up and forced me to change the name to something stupid like Open Regranding.

My nose began to bleed profusely as I crossed the kitchen to check in with Fridge. I figured it had to do with phone signals. I wanted to read what Fridge had to say about my success. I guess I was just looking for validation from my friends. I opened Fridge and found that all of the produce and tofu was gone. There was a solitary jar of olives. I sighed and got a whiff of my own breath.

The jar of olives read:

THOSE NEWSPAPERS

WERE VERY INSIGHTFUL.

UNPLUG ME PLEASE.

What a stain I am.

The Open Regranding was horrible. Fridge didn't provide any food; both Indoor Pumpy and Outdoor Pumpy were pissed at Fridge— they had both developed a thing for Fridge, who wasn't having any of it—and they were pissed at each other for the other being attracted to Fridge.

"Do you have to take rejection to that weird dark place?" I asked them. "Just be cool, dummies. Besides, you're appliances."

APPLY THIS, they said to me with water messages. Pumpy and Pumpy began churning, releasing polluted water into the pools. The pools begin to sizzle and give off a toxic-smelling fume. Swimmers emerged covered in brown gunk. The guests began coughing and gagging, and they stormed out of the building screaming for ambulances and police.

Ruby showed up as the people scurried away in fear. He started telling me he's pretty sure this Weather person Will keeps mentioning is not a person at all, and is the actual weather.

"No duh," I told him. "What's your point?"

Rube kept going on, telling me he's been staking out Santa's motel, watching Will come and go, even following him to the grocery store.

"So, you're stalking him," I said as I set up large fans to blow all of the fumes out of the building.

"I've been keeping an eye on him," he yelled

over the motors and whirring blades. "I thought you'd be proud of me."

"I'd be proud of you," I said, "if you'd rob a bank and buy some groceries. I've blown through the photo album money and I've maxed out the credit cards."

"Sure thing, boss," Rube said. He twirled on his heel and darted toward the exit, slamming into the door. The door had a little placard that read PULL.

Ruby jumped into the passenger side of his car, out of breath, and threw the bag of money into the backseat. I sped off, back to Candy Factory, Ruby going on excitedly about how robbing a bank isn't anything like the movies.

"When is anything ever like the movies?" I asked.

"But here's the weird part," he went on. "When the tellers went into the back and locked the door, this big metal claw came out the ceiling and dropped the bag of money on the counter."

As I drove, I could hear police sirens over the radio. It sounded like all of Tampa was being swarmed by large gas-powered robot bees. Ruby started having a little meltdown and sunk down to the floorboard. I told him to calm the hell down and he started muttering about how he wasn't ready to eat prison food.

"Your taste in food sucks anyway," I let slip out.

Ruby clawed the back of my seat like a cat and it felt like my chest was going to burst as I tried to ignore him and focus on outmaneuvering the police.

"Get back in your seat. What are you, a bunch of half-empty water bottles?"

The sirens grew louder, and I expected an intense car chase. But the chase never happened; things never happen like they do in the movies, except when characters say, "Things never happen like they do in the movies," and then go and spoil the moment by doing something exactly like they do in the movies.

Once we made it back to Candy Factory, I got really paranoid about the car, so I drove it into the patio pool. The pool was still full of shit, so I figured it was the perfect hiding place.

Rube didn't complain about his car. He just kept yapping about his favorite TV show character making a terrible decision in the previous episode. Rube was getting mad about it too. There was genuine red-faced fury in the backseat with me as I cracked open the driver's side window with the safety hammer I had packed away in Ruby's glove compartment. I started to wish driving gloves hadn't gone out of style.

The car bubbled to the bottom and we scrambled to the pool's edge. Rube complained about his character all the way up the stairs into the office.

"Why are you talking like that?" I asked him while I shoved the money in the safe under the desk.

Ruby paced around the office. "I hate him." He was dragging his feet and it was making me hate him.

"Do you get mad at hot fudge sundaes?"

"Sometimes. You know, when they suck."

"Fair enough," I said.

I paid the bills and bought some groceries. I had Jim come out to take a look at the pumps, and that's what he did. He didn't fix them. He just looked at them, got super confused and left. I wrote Fridge a note and slipped it into the crisper drawer. I tried to shut the heavy green door softly. Ruby was leaning on the side of Fridge, looking down at me with an overconfident smile.

"Fridge is done with us," he said. "Give it up already."

"Rube," I said, walking away. "You are not a part of us."

Fridge never responded to that note or the dozen more I slipped it. Ruby kept hanging around while and I considered hurting him a few times for hanging over my shoulder. The office was pretty big and luxurious, but it still felt cramped with Ruby lounging around.

"Don't you have a job?" I asked him one day.

"My parents pay for everything," he said.

"Well, goddammit. You want to be a part of us so bad, why didn't you offer to pay the bills?"

Ruby laughed and kicked his feet, sprawling out on our Deconstructed Chesterfield Collection sofa. We had gone a little overboard with the money and wanted to make the place look like a private investigator's office from the 30s, so we started filling it with furniture from Restoration Hardware. That place is so yuppie, but I love it so much.

"You fucking mooch," Ruby said. "I'm not buying my way in. Even if I did, you would never let it go."

Later that night, I cooked a big batch of pad thai with fried tofu. We ate it on the stairs, looking over the empty restaurant. The water in the pool was still dirty, and had begun swirling on its own accord. After dinner, I watched

Ruby get drunk on cognac and dance around the office, nearly spilling brandy all over the furniture. Ruby passed out on the Chesterfield a couple hours later after pouring all of the liquid into his mouth instead of onto the furniture. I passed out under Will's desk.

As we slept, Pumpy—Indoor Pumpy—became mobile, sprouting PVC legs and walking around the dining room, leaving a trail of dirty water. It went all the way up the rod iron stairs and broke into the office, flooding the room. I was soaked when I woke up. It thudded past us and stole Will's pistol from the top drawer. It went outside and shot Outdoor Pumpy, killing it. Indoor Pumpy went back inside and killed itself, fell into the whirlpool.

In the morning, after a long, awkward period of Ruby and I thinking I had pissed all over the floor, we went downstairs and found the dead pool pumps.

"I guess we need new pool pumps," I said.

The whirlpool of dirty water began to

morph into a whirlpool of millions of tiny wormlike creatures. They oscillated with a bio-luminescent green glow in uneven intervals, like they were trying to communicate with us.

CHAPTER SEVEN
More Like a Laundry Basket

Asshole pool guy Jim informed me over the phone that the worms were a worldwide phenomenon just like the sentient appliances.

"So do I get a refund or what?" I asked.

"No, asshole."

Every night for two weeks, Ruby and I sat in front of the flat screen, got drunk, and watched sweaty, nervous news anchors and senators screech at each other. The media screamed through our screens that the water was unsafe for external and internal human contact. Pundits and politicians told us we would soon all die of dehydration. Everyone kept bathing and drinking anyway. The long-term effects were probably going to be devastating. Ruby and I kept asking why they weren't consulting and interviewing scientists.

After two weeks of sitting around Candy Factory I had had enough, or at least needed a break. Ruby was useless and wouldn't stop putting his feet all over the private investigator furniture. Fridge wasn't writing to me anymore. I had gained twenty pounds of cognac fat.

I drained the outside pool of the worms, built a ramp, and stole Ruby's car. I drove to Treasure Island—which on the way I remembered was Will's favorite book—pulled up to Santa's motel and, after avoiding being attacked by the stray dogs in the parking lot, went into the recreation room and played *The Simpsons*. Halfway through level six I had a craving to play *Zombies Ate My Neighbors* and Santa cleared his throat, scaring me out of the chair.

"Sorry," Santa said and wiped some crumbs —probably cookie crumbs—from his hand onto his red hoodie.

"Jesus Christ," I said. I got up from the floor and sat back down at the game machine.

"You're not staying here for free," Santa told me. "And stop calling me Santa."

"I didn't."

"Damn right. Glad we understand one another."

Santa had errands for me to run; first on the list was picking up Christmas decorations. When I got to Home Depot, I went straight to the back of the warehouse and sniffed the lumber. After an employee with shaggy hair and a little mustache shooed me away, I strolled over to the appliances section. I asked an employee with a fake hand and shaved eyebrows if they had any models connected to the waterline. They had two, so I climbed inside both. I was hoping one of them would take me somewhere. I was pretty pissed when they didn't.

I left without any decorations. I drove all the way home, back to Candy Factory, and arrived to crime scene tape in front of our door;

I assumed Ruby had put it up while I was gone, so I tore it all down and went straight to the office.

I thought about my grandfather for a long time as I sat at Will's desk with my hands folded, staring out the window at the yellow tape spiderwebbed through the entire dining area, from wall to wall, floor to ceiling, around and around. My grandfather had been a cop; he wouldn't have approved of this, and not just the tape. I wrote a note to Fridge. It read:

I MISS YOU.

A couple days later, Fridge left a pack of dark chocolate with a note at the end of the ingredients list, reading:

SORRY I'VE BEEN GONE SO LONG.

DOING WHAT YOU HUMANS

CALL SOUL SEARCHING.

WILL YOU SLIP SOME CHARITY

PAMPHLETS IN MY CRISPER DRAWER?

I remembered a stack of them stashed under the sink of Will's old apartment. I had put them there when we first discovered Fridge's ability, before we became cynical and douchey.

I thought about draining the indoor pool, but I liked the idea of scuba diving to the bottom of Will's apartment. So, I swam to the bottom of the pool through the hole into Will's basement place. The worms had disappeared all on their own. His blessed porn stash and sauce packet collection floated around me. Eventually I reached the sink and pulled out the literature on World Hunger United and One Meal at a Time. Before I swam out of his kitchen back toward the surface I saw a trap door on the floor in front of the kitchen sink. Will's ugly periwinkle kitchen mat floated by; I realized it had always sat on top of the door. I grabbed the inset handle and I pulled without luck. I was going to need to drain the pool. When I got back to the surface I opened the drainage valve and watched the water level fall.

I slipped the soggy pamphlets into Fridge's crisper drawer before I climbed down into the

apartment and opened the hatch. It lead down-
to a grand sewer pipe, big enough to drive a
truck through. I held out my hand and flicked
my thumb forward, attempting to shine my
flashlight through the tunnel. Then I realized
that I didn't have a flashlight in my hand.

After grabbing my survival gear—eating
dead rats and drinking sewer water sounded
unappealing—I went back down into the sewer
and started wandering around down there. I
was down there for two weeks, pretty lost; I was
just glad I brought so much canned corn and
bottled water, and definitely did not voluntarily
eat any dead rats. Eventually I found a Ninja
Turtles-style hangout. It was an old subway car
I found in the section of sewer that I guessed
connected with an old subway system. I wiped
what felt like fur from my mouth, though, like
I said, I hadn't eaten any rats, and stepped into
the car. I'd never known that Tampa used to
have a subway system.

"Tampa never had a subway system," Will

said to me from his dirty old recliner in the cor-ner of the car. "This is part of Treasure Island."

"That's some fucked up city planning," I said to Will.

"Have you been eating rats?" He pointed to the fur on my shirt.

"Have you been living down here?" I tried to be sneaky and empty my back pockets of little not-rat skulls without him noticing. "This doesn't feel real."

"You're in shock," Will said. He grabbed a broom and began to sweep up the bones. "It's a natural response."

Will told me about his travels: how he'd taken this subway system all the way from Treasure Island—which he kept saying in a pirate accent—to Atlanta and back. When I told him that they don't connect, he laughed, told me I was naïve. He offered to let me stay as long as I needed, told me I could sleep on the floor like the dog I was. I took him up on it, and even offered to share my canned corn and bottled water. As he showed me around the car, explaining how he connected electricity to it, showing me all of the dirty furniture he filled it with, muttering the words, "Cold War," over and over, he kept doubling back to his speaker system to continue replaying that song they always use during friendly montage scenes when the characters grow to love each other. We giggled and threw soap suds all over each other as we washed his dishes together in the sink he had fashioned out of a Leslie's Power Powder Pro bucket. I was almost positive it doubled as his toilet.

One night, he forced me to pull out my tent and set it up in the middle of his living room, which was just the middle of the car. I set it up and he told me his deepest, darkest secrets in the dark. He flipped on my flashlight and told me to make shadow puppets. I made a bird, a dog, and a hand; those were the only ones I knew how to make. He promised me he wasn't disappointed, but I was disappointed in myself.

The next morning, while I started making tea, Will got mad at me. He screamed about how much he hated tea and he asked me how tea had even gotten through his security system. I told him I found it in his cupboard. Will jumped on top of me and punched my face; my mouth tasted like blood and Connecticut. The world slipped from me..

I woke up briefly to a scratchy sensation against the back of my head, a tugging sensation at my feet. The sewer ceiling moved in earthworm slinks; Will was holding my feet, dragging me through the tunnels.

I woke up again, this time next to my tent and a fire. Will was roasting some of my vegan hotdogs. He looked at me, spinning the hotdog poker, and smiled.

"Order up," he said, and I heard a bellhop bell ding as I passed out again.

I woke up later to the hot rush of copper flooding my nasal passage. My head hit the dry pool floor.

"Stop!" I yelled and Skibs stopped punching me. His smile faded as he lowered his fist.

"Sorry," he said. "You just never told me to not punch you."

"What are you doing here?" I asked.

"Here to apply for a job at your award-winning restaurant," Skibs said. He took my hand and help me up. I felt malnourished and fuzzy.

"Award-winning?" I said.

Will walked up from behind Skibs, smiling with a customer service smile.

"That's right," Will said. "Award-winning."

For the next week, Will forced me to clean Candy Factory while he sat in his office blasting Lionel Richie's Greatest Hits. I refilled the pools and bought two new pool pumps. I opted for nonliving pumps, but Jim told me there's no such thing anymore as he munched on a bowl of worms. His teeth glowed green.

Will ended up hiring Skibs. He hired Ruby too.

He fired me.

CHAPTER EIGHT
Stonewalling

"You're fired," Will told me.

"Great," I said. I walked back to my apartment that evening, which wasn't my apartment anymore. I found out when I tried the door and it was locked. A hairy guy, completely naked, cracked opened the door and told me he'd lived in the unit for twelve years.

"I didn't forfeit my lease," I yelled at him, punching the blue door as he shut it.

"Didn't say you did."

I punched the door again. The door opened and hairy naked guy rushed me, spinning me around and locking my arm behind my back. We moved in step away from my threshold and

I could feel his chest hair as he whispered in my ear about immediately leaving as soon as he let me go or else he'd cook and eat me.

I didn't want him to do that, so I left, houseless. I thought it was going to turn into some movie-type situation where I'd meet a bunch of houseless guys and we'd heat up baked beans over a fire, but that never happened. Nothing happens the way it does in the movies. I only met one guy named Greg. He told me not to mess with this guy named Ralph. Greg told me that Ralph was an undercover journalist doing an exposé on the houseless.

"He's a fuck," Greg told me.

After three nights of it, I moved into Santa's motel. Santa let me stay for free as long as I agreed to two stipulations: I would stop calling him Santa (I kept calling him Santa), and I would actually complete the chores he assigned me. He sent me back to Home Depot for Christmas decorations and told me not to weird any of the employees out by insisting on calling them Christ Mass decorations. So, I did, meaning I didn't. When I got back to Santa's motel I dropped off the decorations at his office; there was a bag of quarters waiting for me in front of my door. It went on like this for a while: I did his errands, he gave me money, and I spent it all on playing games in the rec room. Things seemed good, like in the movies. But even in the movies the good parts are short and montage-y.

One day, while I played *The Simpsons* in a post-errand haze, a guy in black cloak, claiming to be a member of the Order of the Cacti, slipped me a note. I tried to ask him about it, but he ran away.

The note read:

WILL HAS CREATED A

WEATHER CONTROL MACHINE.

"Is this from Fridge?" I yelled as his cloak flapped sideways in the wind. Except for his red briefs, he was nearly naked.

The Game Over screen flashed its countdown at me, begging for my attention and more of my quarters. And why should I care? This was Will's problem, and his ADD had ensured that none of our problems were unsolvable ones. So he's back at Candy Factory making weather-controlling machines; when that doesn't work out, he'll move on to the next thing—beetle fighting or some such. Nothing he's done before had the potential to be world-shattering, and he's never been very good at follow-through.

The Game Over screen faded away and returned to the Intro screen. I fed the machine more quarters, but the more levels I beat the more I thought of how Will had acted down in the sewers and how quickly he'd taken ahold of Candy Factory, until it turned into a dull ache I couldn't shake. So I ran after the cloaked weirdo, quarter baggie in hand. I found him running around the pool, like he'd been doing laps waiting for me to catch up. The sunbathers gave us weird looks as I chased him in circles. You'd think I would have caught up to him, after all those laps he'd been doing, but he managed to stay ahead of me. So I threw the bag of quarters at his head. This wasn't a rational decision, clearly, but I wasn't thinking rationally or clearly, clearly. That's how I ended up in this whole predicament anyway. I prayed good aim would get me out of it as the cloaked weirdo tumbled into the pool, quarters flying everywhere.

"Hey, asshole," I said, and popped off my shirt. I jumped into the pool, splashing the sunbathers. A few of them got up and headed to Santa's office to complain; the rest watched apathetically, placing lazy bets on us with the quarters.

We bobbed in the water staring each other down for a moment.

"Tell me where the weather thing is," I told him. The sunlight was doing an excellent job exposing his face. He was very pale and gaunt, like a vampire. But I was positive that vampires didn't exist, so I figured he was just a pale, gaunt guy.

He smiled. "We tried to help you. You do not push a member of the Order into a pool." His smile faded away and he whipped out a knife, either from his briefs or the inside of the cloak. I hoped for the cloak option.

A lot of weird shit can happen in a motel pool when a pale wacko in a black cloak is about to stab you. One example: a large, self-conscious man who looks a lot like Santa Claus, wearing a Queen's Night at the Opera shirt in the pool, might jump in front of you and take the hit in the gut.

Which is what Santa did. Three younger Santas, who I could only assume were his sons, rushed onto the patio.

The pale wacko let go of the knife, and Santa floated in my arms gently. Santa's sons jumped in the pool. The apathetic sunbathers remained apathetic. Pale wacko guy smacked the water with both hands.

"Damn tourists," he screamed as Santa's sons grabbed him and pulled him under the water.

Tears welled in my eyes as I looked down at my hero. One of the sunbathers turned up the volume on their boombox, Dave Grohl announcing louder that there goes my hero, watch him as he goes. I rolled my eyes and focused back on Santa. He gave me a sloppy grin and reached out to me, awkwardly touching my face, mostly my eyeballs.

"I just wanted to get my groove back."

I started to cry. I love people who make out-of-date movie references.

The sons never came up. Between the swirls of blood, I saw them swimming underwater, dragging pale wacko guy to a hatch at the deep end of the pool. As paramedics pulled us out I watched as the water level dropped.

Santa ended up being okay. He didn't even lose that much blood. I bought him flowers and brought them to his room. I hung out with him for the day and we watched *Seinfeld* reruns, hours and hours of episodes, a marathon of George Costanza's failures and the abundant lack thereof of triumph.

George never seems to catch a break.

"Florida was the experiment," Santa told me. "Florida was stop number one on the Agenda."

This was the abridged version of his life story. He told me this before proceeding to the unabridged version. It felt rude to stop him, and the abridged version was vague anyway, so I let him explain things.

Born and raised in Tampa, Santa, née George, spent most of his days in the Interbay neighborhood watching *Seinfeld* reruns and wondering about the sewer system. As a kid, he used to walk around his house knocking on walls, convinced he would find a hatch to a room full of gold. His mom got pissed at him one time when he knocked a big hole in the drywall of the laundry room. He was sure there was a TV-trope-sized sewer system beneath Interbay.

After a stint in Colorado—five years of

being a ski instructor in the winter and spring, and a white-water rafting guide in the summer —Santa moved back to Tampa and rented out his old roommate Donovan's mother-in-law suite, at which point Donovan gave him two weeks to find a job. Sony started releasing the *Seinfeld* seasons on DVD right around that time, so Santa spent two weeks watching *Seinfeld*. Donovan wasn't a huge fan of Santa behavior, so he kicked him out. Santa took his Ford Bronco II and moved to Los Angeles, where he tried to get a job with Sony. He wanted to be the guy who pokes the holes in the *Seinfeld* DVDs, but a member of the hiring team explained to him that a machine makes the holes.

After trying to cry on the edge of his dirty motel bed for a few days, Santa drove back to Tampa and got a job as a fry cook at The Improv. He put himself through school with the help of a crippling loan, earned a degree in engineering and did a minor in ancient secret societies. He got himself a job with the military, got commissioned by the state government, and helped design and set up the water delivery systems all over Florida.

"And how'd you get from there to owning this motel?"

He explained to me that he had begun asking the higher-ups too many questions about the Agenda, so they told him to retire.

"The people upstairs are still using my designs for the rest of the country."

"And what kind of gunked-up funk are you guys doing to the water?"

"I can't tell you."

"It's top secret or confidential, or whatever you people say."

"Precisely."

"Where do you stand on the *Seinfeld* finale?"

"I love it," he told me.

"Why do so many people hate it?"

"Why do people like taking selfies? Why does pre-vomit saliva protect our teeth from stomach acid? I can't tell you."

The hospital room suddenly smelled weird, like old baseballs. I was feeling woozy from all the situational comedy and sewer talk. My mouth filled with pre-vomit saliva, which I had just recently found out helps protect our teeth from stomach acid. I grabbed the waste paper basket next to Santa's bed, catching the vomit almost in time, like catching a spider in the middle of biting your hand, meaning I got half the vomit on the floor.

"Gross," he said, throwing his sheet at me. "Are you kidding me?"

I took it and swooshed it around in the puke, trying to scoop it up. I cleaned it up, sort of. We watched eight more hours of *Seinfeld*.

Santa and I became very attached to each other over the next two days. I stayed in his hospital room while he recovered. He told me to leave, but I knew it was just the medication talking. I was stealing his pain pills, so I felt like we were riding the same wavelength.

On the last day, a little before check-out time, his sons stopped by. They gave him flowers—roses I think, which are usually given as a romantic gesture or a flower given after an incredible performance. Santa told them that the "sacred work" was working perfectly. Then, one of Santa's sons noticed me sitting in the corner of the room, or he pretended to notice me sitting in the corner of the room.

"What the fuck is he doing here?" he yelled, or pretend-yelled.

"The asshole won't leave," Santa said. "I think he's houseless."

"Why hasn't the staff thrown him out?" another son asked.

"They haven't checked on me in three days," Santa said. "Not since they patched me up."

Santa's third son shoved his stubby index finger in my face. "Get the fuck out of here." He grabbed me by the shoulders.

"Okay fellas," I said, and squirmed in his

grip. "I get it. This is some elaborate gaslighting campaign. I'll play along."

"Get help," Santa said. "Go to wherever the psych wing is here and get help. 8th floor I think."

"We have secret things to talk about," the first of the sons giggled. "Tantalizing things."

"Dad," the second son said, the one with a shaved head. I felt superficial for noticing this. "I don't think it matters if he stays. He doesn't have the attention span to hear anything beyond the first statement."

"Can I still stay at the motel?" I asked.

Santa's third son looked at me and let go of my shoulders.

"Just stop playing *The Simpsons* game," Santa told me from the hospital bed. "Other guests might want a go."

I plopped back into the chair. My shoulders throbbed from his grip, but I didn't mind too much.

"So," Santa said, his sons turning back to

him. "About system five and the underground: is it ready for the removal of pipe fourteen and its decoy replacement?"

I leaned in. I was excited about the tantalizing secret about to be revealed, but the conversation definitely felt staged for me. Santa kept making exaggerated hand gestures that looked coded; his sons kept making exaggerated facial expressions that also looked coded. The closer I examined the hospital room, the weirder it looked. The bald son caught me staring at the open door, and what looked like the lobby of Candy Factory on the other side, so he quickly shut the door. Then, he winked at me.

I stopped paying attention and tried to remember Candy Factory's address. Sometimes I say my address to myself over and over again, like I'm scared of having a stroke and forgetting. But I didn't have an address any more and I couldn't remember where Candy Factory was; I couldn't tell if I'd forgotten the address because I didn't have a place, or if I didn't have a place because I'd forgotten the address. And this hurt me, but I habitually block out anything that I think might hurt me, for fear of learning to enjoy the hurt and becoming some kind of masochistic sex maniac. So I thought of Will and the old times until it got late and visiting hours were up.

Santa and his sons offered to give me a ride back to the motel. They were very insistent on that fact: that we were going back to the motel. They kept repeating it, even when we pulled onto the highway heading back to the motel. The bald son, sitting next to me in the backseat, was still fiddling with his faulty seatbelt, kept talking about being head of torture and pain. I thought it was a sex thing. I wasn't paying attention though. I was busy thinking about asking Santa about the hatch at the bottom of the pool.

"I want to ask you something," I said, but stopped myself from continuing. Santa wasn't paying attention anyway.

Nothing happens the way it does in the movies—time especially. You can't just jump from one scene to the next like it's hopscotch. But we were on the highway and I didn't remember how we'd gotten there. I knew how to get there, but I didn't remember everything in between being offered a ride and now.

"We're going back to the motel," Santa's sons said simultaneously.

I looked out the window. There was snow all over, and coming down heavy; clusters of Douglas firs whizzed by. The stars outside looked colored, like string lights you'd wrap around trees. I pulled my face from the van's window and noticed that the stars weren't colored like string lights, but that there were string lights wrapped around the windows of the van. The bulbs of the string lights were little models of my severed head. It was snowing inside the van now. Maybe I wasn't in the van anymore.

"Calling me Santa all the time," Santa said. "You motherfucker." The cabin of the van got long, like Will's subway car.

"Are you going to," I said, slurring, "cut stuff off?"

Now I was in the subway car; I felt heavy, like I had walked all the way from the real subway car to the real Candy Factory. And where were my shoes? Now I was positive I was in Candy Factory, that the subway car was just some stage. My haziness mixed with the string lights, spinning and stirring, zigzagging around. The metal poles for standing passengers to grab onto looked far away and huge all at once, and sparkled with bits of color from the overhead lights. I tossed and turned in my seat, which felt rough, like bark, and itched me. I went to scratch my back, and couldn't; my hands and feet were bound with thick, ancient rope. My seat had sunk away; I sat at the base of a massive Douglas fir. Another Douglas fir, decked out in lights, stood where one of the metal poles had been. The tree's bulbs, little molds of my face hanging low and close to my own face, opened their eyes and drew in labored breaths. They begged for help when I begged for help.

"Merry Christmas," we said to each other simultaneously.

Santa stepped in front of the tree, blocking my view of the bulbs. He put his hands on his hips and HO HO HO'd.

"Open your presents, you little bastard," Santa said. His sons dropped beautifully wrapped boxes in my lap. I cried for quite a while; I wanted to open them badly, but my hands were still tied. I could hear the bulbs crying too, while Santa and his sons stared impatiently at me.

"Merry Christmas," I sobbed. I opened the presents with my feet. The paper flew as I jabbed at the colorful boxes with my toes, which were splayed crookedly. One of the sons brought over an intravenous drip, wrapped just like my presents; it was already attached to me. I could feel the drip now, and the dripping of the drip. It was not a pleasant blend. If I were in

the presence of pleasant people, a couple people taking part in the same trip and a couple
trip-sitters, I suppose it might have been pleasant.

The boxes contained a spatula, a box of
noodles, and *The Joy of Cooking*. I broke out
into another crying fit. Ruby emerged from the
darkness, covered in snow, and slapped a hand
on Santa's shoulder.

"I told you," he said.

Santa knelt and slammed his stubby index
finger on the book.

"Open it," he said.

There was a spatula-shaped key carved into
the pages. Santa grunted as he put his hands on
my shoulders. He smiled at me and for a moment he looked like the Coca-Cola Santa with
his rosy cheeks. I thought about how I didn't
want that kind of face when I was old. That
kind of redness usually had to do with alcohol-
ism. He was probably worried that he looked
like me when he was younger as he stared at

my puffy, tear-soaked face full of desperation. That's the look of Western Society Transition, when youthful optimism is slowly replaced with doddery cynicism.

"That key opens a part of Candy Factory you've never been to," Santa said. "New life." Santa slid his hands across my shoulders to my neck. "We're going to take something from inside you." He squeezed my neck. "And we're going to replace it with something better." The bulbs were quiet and began to dim; the snow was going gray. "Then, you're going to Candy Factory for us to get that bastard Will."

My winter wonderland disappeared and everything was nothing—or was it the other way around?

It was nothing like how it is in the movies, at least.

CHAPTER NINE
Vacation All I've Ever Wanted

I don't understand people, especially when they start asking me questions. I guess I don't trust people. I always feel like I'm being interrogated. Everyone, it seems, is constantly framing friendly conversation around some question that's been swimming around in their mind for a while. Maybe it's a question that they've been kicking around with a partner, romantic partner or business partner, in need of clarity, so the conversation during our next hangout is staged. I must piss off every friend I've ever had.

When we were kids, Will was always talking about the weather. It was a common topic of discussion for every Floridian, not just the go-to reserved for stagnated conversation. Adults, old folk, kids—hell, even babies in Florida talked about the weather.

All through high school, Will talked about building a weather machine: how he'd get the funds, how he'd build it, what he'd do with it. I always laughed. Everyone always laughed. He would ask his science teachers questions about weather control and they would tell him to shut his fucking face up—their words, not mine.

When I woke up, I was back inside one of the rooms of Santa's motel. It smelled funky in there. There were bags of garbage and jars filled with weird liquid. The floor was a sea of fast food wrappers. The cream shell lamps and stained bed were as they had been: cream-colored and stained. I hopped off the bed and with each step my feet obtained a new wrapper. The food remnants on the corners were acting like a horror movie glue. I never knew Santa allowed his rooms to get so nasty. His motel might have been old and out-of-date, but he spent tons of money on a round-the-clock custodial service. For a while, the service had been mandatory and ran twenty-four hours a day. He put that to a stop when he started to lose business. Nobody likes it when a member of the custodial staff barges into their room at three in the morning. We're all either sleeping or doing something bad with our hands.

All over the motel room I found sketches of a modified Slurpee machine and a typo-ridden manifesto. I flipped back and forth through the pages. It was a mess. There wasn't a central concern or intention. There was some talk of Weather, but just a general distaste for pleas-antness and chirping springtime birds; the end of the manifesto was just a list of someone's fa-vorite movies. It was mostly a clutter of runny ink, but I knew exactly whose favorite movies they were.

Since my termination from Candy Factory,

I had thought of and missed Will a total of thirteen times. Sometimes I would get mad at Will for having fired me; sometimes I would get happy. This room left me somewhere in the middle. I suspected I was supposed to feel this way. Everything is on purpose when you think really hard about it, everything is random when you don't think about it, and everything is a mix of both when you're rational. Each scan and survey of the room reinforced my cynicism: I was fucked, and this was all staged.

Christmas was flickering on and off in my mind. I was failing to repress it. I touched the front of my crusty, blood-stained jeans and felt the impression of the key, the little spatula-shaped hunk of metal that Santa had given me. The sound of sleigh bells jingled in my mind, or from a hidden sound system. I turned on the room's cathode ray TV. Al Pacino and Diane Keaton were walking across the screen, cheerful, carrying stacks of decoratively wrapped boxes.

"What do you want for Christmas?" Al asked Diane.

"Me?" Diane said. "Oh, just you." She sounded nervous and I felt scared for her. I turned off the TV.

Will taught me how to steal candy in a roundabout way. He would grab chocolate bars and bubble gum from the candy aisle and then walk over to the Slurpee machine. Will would then drop the handfuls of candy into the extra-large cup. He'd turn the knobs and watch the red, green, and blue slush fill the empty spaces between candy bars. After filling the cup and concealing the stolen treats inside, he'd pat the side of the machine and talk about how it was never meant to be a Slurpee machine, how sometimes we all just need some help getting there, to wherever or whatever 'there' was for any of us.

Years after our summer candy sprees, and years after we worked at Sunset Cinemas together, we would sometimes get nostalgic. Well, I would get nostalgic and I would talk about working at that movie theater. Then, I would feel ashamed afterwards. I could never tell if it was because of my childhood, though it probably wasn't. Everybody had a weird childhood and I was thankful that I didn't have a terrible childhood. I more than likely felt weird after the conversations about the theater because I was self-conscious. I didn't want to sound like one of those losers who never stop talking about their high school years. But, look: it was weird. Will was always bad mouthing the movie theater Icee machine to its face. At one point the thing went missing and everyone was convinced that Will had murdered it; they even said 'murdered' instead of 'broke,' which I never understood. A couple weeks later, he demanded that we purchase a Slurpee machine for the concession stand.

Will's manifesto recounted all of this for me, seemed to know exactly how I perceived my childhood and teenageness. I put the pages beneath my legs, where the base of the toilet met the tile, and thought hard about my past. (The seat cover was down; I promise I wasn't doing my thing.) None of that stuff about the Slurpee machine and movie theater sounded right. But as hard as I tried to think back, I wasn't able to recall any memories further back than when Will started going to open mic nights.

The jingling sound came back, though more like a twinkling, from behind the shower curtain. It reminded me of Christmas again. I could hear Santa again; bits of color flashed in my periphery. The tiles felt cold like snow.

"Open your presents, you little bastard."

"I don't want to," I yelled out to no one. I could see Santa shoving holiday cookies in my face. I could feel my heart pounding and my lungs filling with milk as he waterboarded me in his own distinct way. I could taste Christmas. I didn't want more.

The twinkling sound grew to a roar. My

face felt like it was coming loose. I tore open the curtain.

The Slurpee machine from the fake memory sat in the tub and appeared to be running. There was snowy slush twisting about inside: green, red, and blue, a different color for each of its dispensers. The plexiglass window above the dispenser reminded me of a porthole; it was a submarine without Christmas, a submarine I wanted to be inside. I knelt under the blue dispenser, sucked on the nozzle for several minutes, and prayed for diabetes. When I let go and fell back against the side of the toilet, blue slush dripping onto my stupid band shirt, I noticed blinking lights all over the sides of the machine and wires leading off the back into the shower faucet.

I put my head back under the nozzle and prayed harder. This time, I chose red. I forget what flavor red is supposed to be. It just tasted like sugar, and something else—probably cleaning solution.

Even though I was full of good and bad chemicals, I was still incredibly hungry. I called the front desk from the room's wonky old phone, chunky with the same body as a classic rotary phone. Years of use and cigarette smoke had rendered the phone the same color of spoiled cream as the lamps. I wasn't even sure if Santa's motel had room service. Food, I mean. Yes, there was a series of people in white uniforms that went to each room and cleaned, that kind of room service. But why white uniforms anyway? To look sterile? Whose benefit is that for then? Is it a business decision? Of course, nobody would want to stay at a motel where the custodial staff wore dirty outfits, or outfits they didn't subconsciously register as clean, but then why keep the dirty phones? The thought of taking out a huge loan to start a cleaning business sounded like a great idea. I would make the staff wear the traditional white uniforms, with the addition of tiny top hats; I'd call it Clean and Dandy Cleaning Service and More!

My manic behavior was escalating. I needed help and to get out of that motel soon.

Santa answered the phone and told me to fuck off, that he'd be up shortly.

I didn't remember order a vegan burger—I didn't remember ordering anything; I wanted to, but I'm pretty sure I didn't get the chance—but that's what Santa reluctantly brought me. I opened it and a wad of spit dripped off the patty. I ate it anyway, in the bathroom, sitting on the toilet and staring at the Slurpee machine, the manifesto in my burger-free hand and the plate balanced on my knees. It made me miss Will. The blinking lights made me think of treasure. I felt like a pirate from *Treasure Island*—the book, not the resort town. I wondered what would happen if I messed with the knobs and buttons. And why did Santa want me here with this thing? Did he want me to move it to Candy Factory? Was it a Jesus thing? Or was I succumbing to the gaslighting campaign?

I took the key out of my pocket; I looked

at it, then at the empty plate where my vegan burger had just been.

They've really gotten hardcore with the realism of the fake meat, I thought to myself, though the thought could have come from the same secret sound system as the jinging. It creeped me out.

Did I need to unhook these water lines? Maybe I'd call Santa and ask him. I wanted another burger anyway. I was a little scared that asking him would trigger a rage and he'd torture me to death. I wondered if this was how everyone in Pinellas County felt.

I ordered another burger. Santa brought me a grilled vegan cheese sandwich. While I had him in my room, I asked him why he was being so shady about the Weather Machine. He shoved a slice of the sandwich in my mouth so I couldn't talk, put the plate on my lap, and started giving an explanation.

It was hard to understand. I wasn't really listening anyway. I zoned out and started thinking about selfies and that time I was in North Carolina with Skibs and his significant other, Water. We had left Florida to escape Hurricane Irma. Will was going to stay in Tampa, but the thing started turning west. The basement apartment would surely flood. He couldn't make it up to NC, so he drove to Atlanta.

This wasn't a recalled memory; I was reading the manifesto again.

"All we own, we owe to her," I heard Santa say. When I looked up from the pages, Santa was on the other side of the room. His back was facing me, and he was in the corner.

Her name really is Water, though.

While grifting his way through Atlanta as Irma tore its way through Florida, Will stumbled into the old subway system. Will lived down there for months. Eventually he'd found files and files of failed experiments from the Manhattan Project, experiments that had caused members to be expelled. That's where and how Will learned how to build the Weather Machine.

As I read about Will's adventures, I tuned back in. Santa was explaining this same information to me at the same time. There was a lot of boring stuff about a major gaslighting campaign against me, but I stopped paying attention and started reading again.

Maybe we're all obsessed with taking selfies not because we're all narcissists, but because after a while, living one's life solely from behind the eyeballs can become a bit terrifying. It's the same reason we stare at ourselves in the mirror: to make sure we're still there, the character of our life movie.

"Oh, we love the old one," Santa said. He was sitting next to me now on the edge of the bed. I felt some prick in my arm and colors came crashing into my eyes, greens and reds and blues like lightning over snow.

The *Saved by the Bell* theme song used to get stuck in my head all the time. There was a two-week period when this earworm became debilitating. After a series of panic attacks, I was convinced I had an actual worm in my ear. I walked up to The Bunker and sung it to my coworkers. Water thought it was odd and got it stuck in her head that I was sending her a subliminal message. Earlier that morning, she was "saved by the bell," saved from an embarrassing death. She thought I was making fun of her. I was oblivious until one of our coworkers texted me and told me about Water's freakout. I felt bad. I explained that I wasn't being passive aggressive. I'm just easily amused; sometimes I sing stupid songs out loud. It probably has to do with me being nervous about how dumb I am.

On the rainy afternoon, a couple Tuesdays before, Water was sitting at home staring at her full-size Liberty Bell replica. She was thinking about what it is to be a social creature. She had never been great at it, but she was not the worst. She was, of course, measuring herself by the American standards of social grace. She wanted to get better. She read some articles and watched a couple TED Talks, and even read *Don't Sweat the Small Stuff*. She absorbed as much information as she could. She used this information in real life and it failed; she realized nobody else had all of this information on social grace organized like she did, that everyone else was bumbling around just like her. So she went back to her old ways and it worked.

A couple nights later, during a dinner party, she knocked over a glass of tap water, which people on TV say you should never do. The water splashed onto a stack of her social studies books and they instantly burst into flames. The flames caught her shirt sleeve on fire and the fire quickly grew across her shirt. In a knee-jerk reaction, she jumped out of her chair, and whacked into the Liberty Bell display behind the dining room table.

Water crashed to her tile floor and the full-size Liberty Bell replica landed directly on top of her, instantly putting out the fire. The guests pulled the bell off her, extinguished the flaming books. She walked away from embarrassment unscathed.

CHAPTER TEN
Oh We Loathe the Old One

There was no one by the motel pool to hear any of my loud opinions. I sat down on one of the Adirondack chairs and pretended to smoke. The chair was leaning too far back, so I raised the back and locked the slat in place. I quit seriously smoking a little over a year ago, but the urge to smoke still comes and goes. Sometimes I smoke an invisible cigarette; sometimes I shove a twig in my mouth.

The sun was out. I was surprised that there was no one out by the pool. Maybe everyone was down on the beach.

There was no one down there. For a moment, I thought that there must have been another mass water contamination somewhere in the world and that everyone was watching the news, but then a butterfly fluttered by and I forgot what I was thinking about.

I ventured back to the motel room, forgot to turn on the news, and took a nap. The Weather Machine continued to blip and beep. The blipping and beeping entered my dream. I dreamt that I unhooked the Slurpee machine and its wires and hoses connected to my body, embedded themselves under my skin, into my spinal cord, its living fluids dripping everywhere, grossing out members of the custodial staff. The Slurpee machine unfolded and unlocked itself into various cubes and interlinking formations, all spinning and shifting, closing in on me while I tried telling it about my trip to North Carolina and my fake smoking. It encased me like a mech suit.

A series of loud knocks interrupted my storytelling time; I told the Slurpee machine to hold on a sec. Each knock was different.

There was a jingling rattle, a clattering racket; one knock sounded like hundreds of sick dogs falling down a staircase. I answered the door. It was room service: a woman and a young boy. Their uniforms were traditionally white and immaculate, their tiny top hats clean and dandy.

The woman stared at me blankly. I tugged on my left ear twice. She crossed her arms and the straight line of her mouth tilted down to one side. I smiled to flag my joke. She didn't laugh.

"You could've called," the kid said. He looked about four and I found his words both adorable and sad. I was going to apologize, but stopped myself, realizing how insulting that would've been. The woman smelled my breath and my body. I smelled bad, but I didn't smell like booze. There were no bottles scattered among the piles of Will's garbage.

She dragged me out of the hotel and into a car, told me her name was Lavender, said we needed to eat, that the kid would take care of the mess. On the way, she told me about Candy Factory, about its remarkable success, how it had been written up in all the big magazines.

"Even the celebrity chef from Smash Mouth did an *I Eat, You Starve* episode on it," she told me.

I wondered how Will was sleepcooking without booze.

At a diner, an older couple sitting in the booth next to us was bickering. The man was wearing a red hat. He kept telling his wife he was going to pull out his gun and start executing people. His wife kept talking him out of it. He told her it was his constitutional right to kill everyone in the diner.

After the meal, Lavender drove me to Candy Factory. Before I got out of the car, I asked her if she had noticed anything about the water recently. Lavender ignored the question and told me to finish doing what I needed to do. My stomach hurt, and I told her about the pain.

She told me if something was making me feel shitty then I was probably on the right track. I stepped out of the car and they drove away. As the car pulled up the intersection it became a single panel of unpainted drywall, turned the corner and crumbled. I thought about the diner's kitchen staff, about whether the cooks kept slipping notes into their refrigerators.

The lobby was unguarded, so I did an obnoxious victory dance. But what was the victory? I peeked my head into the dining room. Colleen was right: it really did look like the train station from that Prince music video. It was like a fern bar, but with lots of purple lighting, fake fog, and frosted glass instead of fake Tiffany stained glass.

The restaurant was packed, every chair occupied; servers speed-walking while holding trays aloft. The indoor pool was gone, cemented over; I guessed that the outdoor pool was gone too. Will looked busy in the office, shuffling back and forth across the window, throwing pots and pans at the line cooks. I looked around for a door I had never noticed before.

These days, I find it hard to trust my perception. I've been locked up inside a mental health facility before. My bunkmate was quiet and spacy-looking. My first thought was that he took way too much LSD. Two adults entered our room, introduced as visitors. I was positive that they were his parents and that they were checking up on their temporarily crazy son. They gently smiled at him, said nothing, and left a minute later. But I created that narrative. Maybe his actions were not as cute and innocent as jumping in a pool with a bathing suit full of blotter paper. Maybe he did something violent. Maybe he still jumped in a pool. Maybe that man and woman weren't his parents. Maybe they were going to stay longer, but maybe the way they felt with me in the room, my eyes darting, watching their every move, scared the shit out of them. So they fled. It's all about perspective. If every point of view differs, is there one truth? In most cases, yes, definitely.

And still, it is in my opinion that becoming a premium psychopath is a wonderful way to attain the combination of the formless states. It's like watching movies from every time period and not only being able to intuit various camera techniques and style trends—why those techniques and styles were perfect for that time period in that part of the world, recognizing an understanding of the psychological temperament of whole scores of people, and how those scores of people collectively react to subtle things—but also being able to recognize the flow and connections of those temperaments.

And still, sometimes I get so far into something that it makes me sick. Some days, these things and my mood swings throw me so low that I'm convinced happiness is a mind-control device brought down by demons to trick me into letting my guard down, in order to let every single person I know kill me. But then I remind myself that I'm hypoglycemic and eat a pancake, and the feeling passes. I can only imagine how people in underdeveloped parts of the world feel every day.

What doesn't pass is the feeling you get from knowing that all of the tech support associates of your cell service providers place bets on which kind of porn you watch.

I found the door. Behind the bathroom, down a dark hallway I'd never noticed before was a large red wooden door surrounded by an ornate frame, wisps of gold vines branching off of the solid white background. The door was shining bright, even though I could see no lights pointed at it.

I pulled out the key and slipped it into the keyhole. It made me uncomfortable. The blinking lights of the Slurpee machine framed Will, standing there, smiling with his arms crossed, like a flying saucer. Next to him were the walls of Santa's hospital room on wheels, scattered next to one another like giant playing cards.

Yards away in the corner, I noticed the Christmas decorations from the torture room. Behind the machine was the massive sewer tunnel, disassembled into short pipes stacked next to one another. The center pipe contained the subway car. I was expecting at any moment to spot Santa's motel and the beach, complete with a lighting system to mimic daylight.

"Oh wow," I said to Will. "I wasn't expecting you to be here, standing in front of the Slurpee machine, smiling, with your arms crossed."

Will punched me in the chest, and I punched him back. After one more unenthusiastic punch each he explained the nature of things to me and I had trouble paying attention. Ruby was on the couch in the back of the office, whittling a spatula.

"I didn't even know Ruby could whittle," I said to Will. "You think you know a guy."

"Get down here with me," Will said. He was on his hands and knees. I joined him and we crawled to the Slurpee machine. We pressed all the machine's buttons.

"We've done it," he said calmly. "We've wrecked the planet."

"I don't think so," I told him, tears streaming down my face. I laughed uncontrollably.

Will escorted me to the dining room and made me sit at one of the tables. He prepared an okay meal; it wasn't as good because of his lack of drinking, but it was still pretty good. It's hard to mess up vegan grilled cheese sandwiches anyway.

Skibs and Ruby joined us. It felt like a mafia meeting, like I was a gangster from the rival gang and they were schmoozing me right before shooting me in the back of the head. I got claustrophobic and thought about running, but decided I didn't want to be shot in the back while cowering away. So I decided instead to slip under the table.

If you ever see someone react severely to something you can't see or something that seems insignificant, they might have PTSD.

Curled around the table stem, I caught the

sight of the hatch under my chest on the table base. I thought about opening it. As I reached for the handle, and as Skibs and Ruby rambled on about old episodes of *Saturday Night Live*, I imagined dystopian troopers in solid black armor and face masks carrying intense looking machine guns busting into Candy Factory. I imagined them taking us away to a secret government building and charging us at a military tribunal with the destruction of the world.

There was a dream I remembered having. From 1985 to 2011, every lead guitar part from every song ever made was performed by Tom Cruise making guitar noises into a microphone from behind a curtain. In this dream, I was a bass player for Guided by Voices. The drummer was a dystopian trooper and Robert Pollard was Robert Pollard. During our impromptu performance of "My Valuable Hunting Knife," a rowdy fan jumped on stage and ripped the curtain down, exposing Tom making the lead guitar noises. The crowd broke out into a riot and I was knocked unconscious when I fell off the stage.

Still inside the dream, I woke up to the dystopian trooper drummer standing over me, shoving a vial into the special compartment in their jacket. The trooper noticed me and took off their helmet. It was Santa; it was weird to not see him in a hospital gown or his Queen's Night shirt.

He dragged me all the way back to Candy Factory. The asphalt and brick of the roads scraped the back of my head, leaving a bloody trail behind me. I tried to bring this up with Santa, but he told me I was hallucinating. Dark red clouds receded and exposed the bright blue horizon. I guessed the machine and its temporary effects had been a ruse and I was just like that stupid Slurpee machine: a modified tool.

People were coming out of their houses, shielding their eyes with their hands and peering at the sky. The children ran out into the yards and started playing. I must have been hallucinating; who still plays outside?

Candy Factory appeared as a vision of heaven. Santa pushed open the pearly gates and the hinges screeched. The iron doors of Candy Factory opened with an even more painful creak and I felt like a Manchurian soldier returning home.

Skibs and Ruby greeted me in the lobby. Skibs set a bouquet of lilies on my chest on top of my folded hands. The flowers toppled over into my armpit. Ruby walked with the cart, reached under my hands, and took them. We teared up as we talked to each other without words. It was pathetic, but I kind of liked it. Santa stopped pulling the cart and spun it around, revealing Will, who had his arms crossed. He was smiling. He didn't say anything. I sat up and he shifted to the right, revealing Santa's sons sitting at the table on the edge of the dining room and the lobby, that sacred line between introduction and service. It was the same table I found myself daydreaming under. I could see

Santa walk to the table, each son hunched over in his chair, staring at me hugging the table stem. I saw myself slink back up into my chair. Will stood up and walked around to Santa, taking place behind him. I was sure that Will was about to execute Santa gangland style, but he didn't. He grabbed Santa's shoulders and lightly massaged them.

"Thank you," Santa said, "for your cooperation."

"I didn't cooperate," I heard myself respond. "I kind of just existed."

I still thought Will was going to blow Santa's head off, but he didn't. Will released his hands from Santa's shoulders and walked away, up the stairs into his office kitchen. The door slammed and echoed across the massive factory. Santa stood up, and did not rip his beard off like I thought he was going to. He simply touched his nose as he winked at his sons. His sons touched their noses and winked at him. It looked like they were posing for a Norman Rockwell painting. I laughed loudly at this, and played it off like I was laughing at a joke I was telling myself by shifting my line of sight just past the Santa family at an indiscriminate section of factory wall. Santa took no notice as he picked up his briefcase, which was probably filled with cookies. His sons did not follow suit and stand. They remained seated and viciously ate their meals: squirming masses of glowing worms.

Santa walked away, nodding at the window of the office kitchen and then to Skibs and Ruby, silently saying, "Gentlemen."

I crawled under the table and thought of the line from *Citizen Kane* when Boss Jim Gettys says, "I am not a gentleman. I don't even know what a gentleman is."

And my seat was empty now. Where had I gone off to?

"Have you noticed anything about the water?" I asked Ruby and Skibs, climbing out from under the table, taking my seat—again?

Ruby and Skibs, standing at either side of

me, looked at each other, frowning.

"You should talk to Will about that," Ruby said. "What did you do with my car?"

Skibs poured some sparkling water and invited Rube to sit down. Rube sat and then he sat. I took a sip of water and then took a good, hard look at Candy Factory. Colleen was right: it did look like the train station from that Prince music video.

"Good sparkles," I said to them.

"I would never drink city water," Skibs said. "That shit is poison."

"Like the band," I said.

"Like the toxic substance," Rube said.

People change. Faces change. But nothing felt or looked quite right anymore. Important things looked out of place. Trivial things were all out of whack. Facial construction eluded me. Was one the normal number of noses? Were they supposed to be in the middle of the face or where those weird eyeball things were? Things slipped, but then they returned. It still happens today, but it regulates me, so true slipping doesn't happen as often. I'm still not entirely sure about the basic stuff and I'm not sure if that stuff ever slipped me.

"I'm hungry," I told them and stood up. "I'm going upstairs."

"Don't do that," Rube said.

"Boss doesn't allow anyone up there anymore," Skibs said.

I went anyway, the iron stairs clanking with each step. All the noise should've alerted Will. If he really didn't want me to come up he would've opened the door by now, probably killed me, but he didn't so I opened it for him and remembered how much I loved the kitchen office. Will had added more Restoration Hardware furniture since my firing. He was sitting on the Neoclassical upholstered stool next to his desk, hunched over a cardboard bucket, going to town on some dish.

I was still anticipating Will to kill me, but he didn't. Whatever he was eating was gloppy

and gray, and he was mumbling about hypo-
glycemia. Will looked up from his bucket at me
briefly. He stood up and walked the bucket to
his desk. I thought about using this brief break
in his muttering as an opportunity to talk about
my mania, but decided against it again. There
was no use. Will never listened to anyone. Every time I'd ever tried to talk to him, he'd stop
paying attention a second in and start playing
with one of his collectible Charlie Brown vinyl
figurines. I wasn't resentful about it though. He
didn't have to listen to me and those figurines
are pretty neat. I guessed I should be asking
him about himself instead of talking about myself. He sat down and took the silence as per-
mission to continue stuffing his face.

I asked him how he was doing, but then got
mad at myself for not getting to the point, about
all this *Manchurian Candidate* shit. Will looked
up at me and wiped the sauce off his face with
his shirt sleeve. A headache was building. It felt
chemical, like bleach. I thought about turning

into a garbage person, jumping into a landfill and letting myself sink under the trash, and then under the crust of the Earth.

Will cocked his head. "Why are you looking at me like that?"

"You used me."

"So?" Will said. "Besides, this was your plan."

I felt watched. I turned around. The open mic audience was standing along the window in a row. I don't know how. There's no platform in front of the window. I walked up to it.

"Careful," Will said.

The people were floating; Susy, Tex, Linda, and the rest were smiling at me.

"You're like one of those people who read the back of the incense stick box," Will said.

I turned and shrugged at him, leaving the impossible behind me.

"I'm so full," Will said. "I have never been so full in my entire life."

"Where do we go from here?" I asked Will,

as if leaving was not an option. I sat down at the chair on my side of the desk. It wouldn't have been weird if I had sat down next to him or on top of his desk, but that's not what I did.

Will pointed at the bucket, offering it to me. I declined. I was ready to go home, wherever home would be next, and I did not want to delay getting back by eating tainted food.

"You started this," Will said. "Not me. I just followed through."

"I'm having trouble believing what I'm perceiving."

"Most people do," Will said. "It's a part of the human condition. Get some sleep." He smirked at me, the way he smirked at his vinyl figurines.

"Can I get some food?" I asked. "Real food."

"I don't sleepcook anymore," Will said. "I quit drinking."

"Good for you, but I just want a sandwich or something."

I looked down at the clothes draped across

my weary body. I didn't recognize them. For a moment, it looked like the clothes were made of bunched-up wigs instead of denim and cotton. Will stood up and made his way toward the pantry.

"Have you noticed anything about the water?" I finally decided to blurt out. I was so nervous that my voice cracked. Will backed up out of the pantry, head turned toward me.

"Why are you talking like that?" he said with a look on his face.

I knew I shouldn't have said anything. To Will, this either appeared to be my breaking point or it was all a part of his gaslighting campaign. This is what the higher-ups do to assassins: fuck them up, send them on their way, and make them feel crazy if the truth slowly seeps back in. I guess there's some humanity in that. It's sort of considerate. It's not death. I swiveled around in my seat. The audience was gone. I stood up and walked to the window. The restaurant didn't look like the Prince music video anymore.

"Did you change the lighting?" I asked.

Will yelled from the pantry, "What?"

"Candy Factory doesn't look that one Prince music video anymore, like the train station."

Skibs and Ruby were still below at the table. They looked up at me and waved. Santa came out of the bathroom. With one hand he flipped me off; he made a finger gun with the other, and when he acted as if he had fired it his finger made the sound of a real gun going off and I cowered, ran into the pantry and shut the door.

"You guys really messed me up," I said from inside the pantry, sweat pouring down my face, heart beating out of my chest. "Can you spare me the suspense?"

Ruby opened the doors. He held the spatula right up to my eyeballs; in the handle he'd carved the words MIS EN PLACE.

"It says 'missin' place.' It's French," he explained. "It means that eventually everyone loses everything."

"You've lost me. I don't mean that post-ironically."

"It's simple," Will said from his desk. There was a jar of salsa and liquid cheese, and two eggs on top of the desk. "You told me you were bored. You wanted to shake things up." He played with the eggs, spinning them like tops. "You told me to spike your food with some of the old factory candy."

I chewed on this information for a moment.

"But did I give you the go-ahead?"

"You planned all of this."

"Why would you do this to your friend?"

"I'm not your friend," he said, stopping the eggs gently. "I'm your boss. But first I was your chef. You hired me. You hired all of these people."

"Is that the truth?"

"Maybe, right?" He smiled.

I was not taking anything. Whether this was the truth or not, it was terrifying. I knew it would ruin me. Anything but silence on the subject was too much.

"Did I do something to the water?"

Will's smile became so wide that it ceased to be a smile. It was vulgar, and I could barely keep eye contact. "I've got a new recipe for Candy Factory," he said. The smile died, and his face morphed into a sufferable form. "You want to try it?"

"Are you messing with me?"

"No. I want to try this recipe on you." Will picked up the salsa, the liquid cheese, and the eggs. "I thought I'd lose the ability to cook if I quit drinking, but I think I'll be alright."

Will dropped the bowl on the ground and waved me over to the other side of his desk. He knelt and popped open the jars. He dumped the salsa and cheese into the bowl, his tongue in the corner of his mouth, and then cracked the eggs on top of the salsa cheese slop.

He looked up at me, eager, and smiled.

He handed me the bowl. I didn't want to be rude again, so I took it and slurped down every drop.

ACKNOWLEDGEMENTS
Something Was Done
To the Water

I would like to thank my son Damian; Josh, Joe, Kyle, Eric, Yadi, Sarah, Kevin, Randy, Nick, and Evan from Long Day Press; my soulmate sunflower goddess Christina; Scott, creator of the cheese salsa egg slop; Jill, Ben, Kate, Karen, Sky, Dahlia, Altus, and Kai from La France; Richard and Sam from Gyrojets; my ex-wife and mother of our child, Amy; the incredible artist Ken Echezabal; and the personification of synchronicity, which is probably a dude made out of a bunch of eyeballs. Thank you mom and dad. Thank you Grandma Mary Lou. And thank you Uncle Kenny for introducing me to *Ghostbusters*. Thank you to the band Candy Bars for "The Flood in your Old Town." Thank you Tim Kinsella shifting my consciousness.

ABOUT THE AUTHOR

Florida Man Writes Bizzare Novel, Nothing Bad Happens

Chase Griffin is a novelist and short story writer from the sunny Florida Man haven of Florida. He's published stories in FIVE:2:ONE magazine and Florida Is A Verb. For work, he sells hats. Like old timey hats. Seriously. When he's not clacking away at his laptop or asking about brim width preferences he's making bedroom pop, which can be found at chasegriffin.bandcamp.com. He lives Tampa, a place known for manufacturing the most pointless smokable tube things: cigars.

NOTES

A HEAD FULL OF DREAMS
JAMES ARDIS

"She's superficial and raw and hurting and smart and out of control, and emotional and in pain and striving to find herself."

—Elizabeth Ellen, author of *Person/a*

DON'T NOD

poems

rebecca van laer

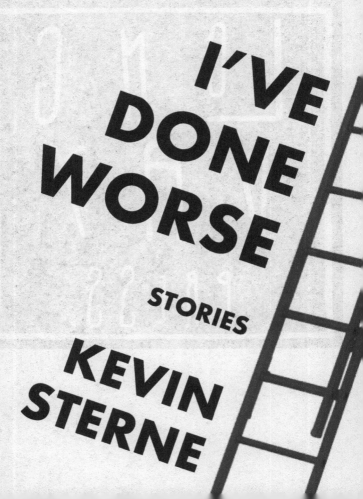

I'VE
DONE
WORSE

STORIES

KEVIN
STERNE